About the Author

Addie Mattox is a semi-retired business consultant who loves to travel, read, write, play duplicate bridge and teach and play pickleball. She holds a graduate degree in English as a second language from UCLA. She is a native Californian who grew up in Pasadena. She and her husband live in the Bay Area.

Dedication

To the three women I love best:
Denise, Andie and Kati

A huge thank you to Loc Barns, my treasured friend and
inspiration for this novel

Addie Mattox

Saigon USA

AUSTIN MACAULEY
PUBLISHERS LTD.

A CIP catalogue record for this title is available from the British Library.

ISBN 9781786295569 (paperback)
ISBN 9781786295576 (hardback)
ISBN 9781786295583 (eBook)

www.austinmacauley.com

First Published (2017)
Austin Macauley Publishers Ltd.
25 Canada Square
Canary Wharf
London
E14 5LQ

Acknowledgments

Saigon USA is a work of fiction. None of the characters are real, but their stories are based on interviews with Vietnamese Americans who were gracious enough to share their experiences with me.

I am particularly indebted to Loc Barnes who inspired this novel. Her family had been encouraging her to document her courageous and successful life. She is far too busy with her real estate business and volunteer work to become an author and accepted my suggestion that I write her story.

I completed Loc's biography as a separate manuscript, but during that writing I became so riveted by the entire Vietnamese experience that I decided to write *Saigon USA*. I wanted to reach a larger audience so they could better understand what Vietnamese boat people and other immigrants went through on their way to becoming proud and productive Americans.

Saigon USA includes selected events from Loc's life along with liberal doses of my imagination and input from other Vietnamese Americans - especially Tony T whose story and love of the U.S. appear throughout this book.

I'm so grateful to my dear friend, Connie Greaser, retired publisher, for her tireless help and invaluable suggestions. Janet Kinney spent hours helping me with graphics and computer painting my young hero. Thanks so much to my friends who read and proofed my manuscript: Robbee Royce, Jean Tuemmler and Daisy Lennon.

A heartfelt thank you to the inspirational Vietnamese immigrants who shared their stories with me.

Contents

Chapter 1 – Bullies   11

Chapter 2 – Faculty Conference   19

Chapter 3 – Tran   27

Chapter 4 – Cam's Story   33

Chapter 5 – Karate and a Party   38

Chapter 6 – Lien's Story   49

Chapter 7 – Tran and Callie   54

Chapter 8 – Faculty Meeting and Lien's Story   62

Chapter 9 – Tran   68

Chapter 10 – Planning International Day   78

Chapter 11 – Cam's Story   86

Chapter 12 – Buddy and Tran   93

Chapter 13 – Cam and Ha   98

Chapter 14 – International Day   103

Chapter 15 – Recovery   111

Chapter 16 – Sundays   119

Chapter 17 – Cam's Story   126

Chapter 18 – Lien's Story   132

Chapter 19 – Pasadena   137

Chapter 20 – The Reunion   142

Chapter 21 – Thao's Story 147

Chapter 22 – Uncle Ba 155

Chapter 23 – Pickleball On Day Three of the Reunion 166

Chapter 24 – Auntie Kim 172

Chapter 25 – Final Day of the Reunion 181

Chapter 26 – Chi's Story 195

Chapter 27 – Dan 203

Chapter 28 – Home 214

Chapter 29 – Lien's Story 221

Chapter 30 – Law School 227

Chapter 31 – Back to California 235

Chapter 32 – South Pasadena 243

Chapter 33 – Decisions 255

Chapter 34 – Lien's Story 264

Chapter 35 – Moving 271

Chapter 36 – Shelley's Story 283

Afterword 284

Chapter 1

Bullies

I was power-walking (there's no running in hallways) from my classroom to the principal's office for our weekly faculty brownbag lunch when I heard chairs crashing against the wall and the ominous thud of a body hitting the ground. Then came the girls' screams over the braying laughter of boys when they know something's not really funny.

Running now, I burst into the cafeteria and found chaos. A group of boys stood over an inert body. A couple of them were high-fiving. The girls clustered together, and one continued to scream.

The boy on the floor wasn't moving, his eyes shut tight. His hands covering his face. Blood was seeping between his fingers.

I tried to ask calmly. "What's happening here?" No answer. I raised my voice, "Girls, please be quiet." I glared at the boys who shrugged and looked away, stifling their smiles. I felt my face burning, my heart pounding and the sweat trickling down my back. I shouted at the boys: "I asked what happened, and I expect an answer." I knelt down next to the silent, bleeding boy.

He was a new student recently transferred to our school as a seventh-grader. I knew he was Vietnamese, but didn't know his name since he was not in my English class. "Are you hurt?" I asked gently. No response. I repeated louder. "Are you hurt?" No answer. I practically screamed at the boy, still curled on the floor, eyes shut. "Shall I call 911?" A tiny voice whispered, "No. I'm Okay."

I stood up and confronted the boys, barely controlling my rage. Through clenched teeth I spat out: "I'll ask again, what happened here?" The boys looked from one to another, shuffled their feet and shrugged. "Then I'll call the principal to ask you. Perhaps you'll explain the situation to him. Or maybe the police." I saw alarm wipe out the smiles on two of the boys' faces.

I turned to a leggy girl who was watching the scene, "Carley, please go to Mr. Picket's office and ask him to come immediately." My voice was shrill and my hands were shaking as I turned back to the boys. "No one leaves this room." Instructions about confronting a bear flashed through my mind, and I tried to look as huge as possible, blocking the exit to the cafeteria. It seemed to work because the boys slowly sunk back to their seats at the table.

Carley was a sprinter on the track team and shot off down the hall. In moments, Mr. Picket burst into the cafeteria, flushed from his jog down the corridor.

"Not again!" he boomed when he saw who the trouble-makers were. "Miss O'Neil, please take Tran to the nurse's office." I saw him turn deliberately toward the table of delinquents.

I tried to help the boy up from the floor, but he shrugged me off. Before accepting the clean towel to stanch the blood pouring from his nose and mouth, he muttered loud enough for the bullies to hear, "Idiots! I'm not even Chinese. I'm Vietnamese." He followed me from the cafeteria, eyes cast down, refusing my offer of a helping hand.

I heard Mr. Picket's purposefully calm voice demanding: "Buddy, tell me what happened."

Then Buddy's whine, "He's a chink. He tried to sit at our table and opened his bag of gross smelling food. We told him to take off, but he just sat there, eating. I told him again, but he pretended not to hear and just kept eating his foreign junk. That's when Mike tossed a chair at him. Not hard, just to get his attention. The chink tossed it back and all hell broke loose."

That's all I heard before leading Tran down the corridor to the nurse's office.

Mr. Picket called an emergency faculty meeting for the following day to discuss the incident.

******

13

When Tran arrived home the day of the attack, he slipped quietly through the back door and was on the stairs when his cousin, Thu, called him. "Tran, you home?"

"Yes, I have a lot of homework tonight. I'm going to my room to study."

"No hungry today like every day?" she called.

"No, not today. See you later." Tran could feel Thu's bewildered expression because he was starving every day after school. He couldn't face her just yet and knew she would not insist on a conversation if he had homework. His cousins were committed to his earning all As.

He took the stairs two at a time and quickly closed the door to his room, a sure sign he didn't want to be disturbed. He looked in the mirror for the first time since the attack and winced when he saw his left eye, already half shut, circled by purplish skin. His shirt and jeans were bloodstained. Thu would certainly notice these when she did the laundry.

There was no way to hide his damaged face. He just didn't feel like talking about it now. He knew he'd have to explain what happened at dinner. Why go through it twice?

He lay on his bed and pulled his arm across his eyes, hoping to block out the day. It didn't work. The boys' laughter rang in his head and he saw their mean, twisted faces as they told him to "get lost, chink."

He was only following his cousin Tony's advice: "Sit down at their lunch table and don't say anything. They will get used to you. Soon they will think of you as their friend." Tony obviously had no idea about American boys. How could he? He went to school in Saigon.

The humiliation of being told to get lost was far more damaging than being thrown against the wall. His body would heal, he knew, but how was he going to face the boys the next day? And the girls who screamed? He had no answers.

He was doubly upset that Hanna was sitting at the next table when the problem started. He thought she was the prettiest girl in seventh grade and dreamed about dancing with her at the class party, even though he didn't know how to dance. He had never spoken to her, but he tried to sit near her in the two classes they had together. He doubted she would recognize him if he were the only boy in the room. That is, until today. She'll recognize him tomorrow, that's for sure. For all the wrong reasons.

Two hours later, Thu gasped when Tran entered the kitchen. "What happen to you?" Thu's voice was strangled. Her brother, Tony, rushed into the kitchen when he heard his sister's cry. Tony stood in the doorway, quietly waiting for Tran's explanation.

"Nothing serious. Just a problem with some stupid boys," he said dismissively. "What's for dinner?"

Tony stared intently at Tran and asked quietly, "I want to know what happened. We will eat dinner after we talk."

Tran knew there was no distracting Tony when he had that serious look on his otherwise mild face. He drew in a breath and told his cousins an abbreviated version of the story. They were calm, but their faces fell with disappointment, then switched to confusion.

Tony turned to Thu, "How can we help Tran?" His voice was pleading and frightened at the same time. Tran knew his cousin would do anything for him. He also knew that Tony had no experience with teenage American girls or boys. The most Tran could expect from his cousins was sympathy. And maybe, he thought, that's enough.

Tran spoke quietly to his cousins and met their eyes for the first time since entering the kitchen. "I'm an American. I can handle school. I can deal with the boys who hate me because I don't look like them. They are nothing compared to what you and my parents have gone through for me. Don't worry about me. I'll be fine." Tran knew to keep his language simple.

Thu had taken ESL classes, but her vocabulary was limited. Tony's English was fluent because he worked with Americans in a shoe factory.

For a brief moment, Tran imagined having a conversation where he could pour out his heart to them about loneliness, about not feeling part of either the US or Vietnam, about missing his parents, about his uncertain future, about the chances of never seeing his father again. He wanted to tell them about Hanna, the gorgeous girl with the blonde ponytail who wouldn't even look at him in math or history. About his dream of asking her to the year-end dance.

The phone startled them. It rarely rang. The cousins exchanged worried glances, sharing their fear about bad news from Vietnam. Tony answered with a quiet hello. His placid face clouded and he said, "Yes we can come tomorrow afternoon." A short pause while he listened. Then, "Yes, Tran can come with us. I understand, we will meet in the principal's office. Tran will show us where to go. Thank you. Good-bye."

Tony turned slowly to the two expectant faces. "That was the school secretary. We will meet with the principal and a teacher tomorrow afternoon." Tony took a deep breath. "Now tell us everything that happened today. Do not be afraid. We know you are a good boy." Tran gave a more detailed description of the incident.

Thu offered, "You did nothing wrong. The boys are bad. I am sorry for you. This happens in a new country."

Tony appeared to be gathering his thoughts. He finally said: "There aren't many Asian people in this town." Tran waited expectantly for his cousin to continue, but that was all he said. They ate dinner in silence, then Tran excused himself to finish his homework.

Tran usually fell asleep within minutes of going to bed. Not tonight. His legs tangled in the sheets in

17

frustration as he twisted from side to side, chewing over the questions he'd been asking himself since September. How can I make the kids accept me, even like me? How can I get Hanna to notice me? What if Tony and Thu tell my mother what happened today? She'll be so disappointed. She's counting on me to save our whole family in Saigon. What if the principal decides I'm responsible for what happened? How will the boys ever accept me if the principal punishes them? Would it be better to say I started the fight? Maybe that would make them let me sit at their lunch table. I wish, I really wish, there was someone I could talk to. Not an Asian person. An American who would know what I should do.

He slept fitfully that night. The bruises under his eye morphed from purple to yellow, not too noticeable against the color of his skin.

Chapter 2

Faculty Conference

The atmosphere in the conference room early the next morning felt as welcoming as the freezing air in Costco's produce section. Not even the aromatic croissants I'd picked up at La Boulange lightened the somber faces of my colleagues. Mr. Picket looked gray and grave. Based on my own restless night, I suspected he had slept badly or not at all.

He began, "It's 1990 according to the calendar, but it seems more like fifteen years ago. I was a brand new math teacher in a small town in Indiana. The local church had sponsored a large family from Saigon, and their kids attended our school. I think they were the first Vietnamese people our community had ever seen." No one coughed or shuffled or dug into handbags or briefcases as he spoke.

He continued in a sad, low voice that everyone strained to hear.

"The war was over. The North Vietnamese communists had won. The US had pulled out. All the South Vietnamese people who could, had escaped. Who knows what happened to the ones who remained." He closed his eyes and was quiet for a few seconds, then shook his head slightly.

"I didn't call this meeting to discuss history. Miss O'Neil, please summarize what happened yesterday."

I was startled to be called on, but gave a brief description of the incident. My colleagues had obviously heard about it, since they didn't ask any questions.

Mr. Picket addressed me again: "Do you have Vietnamese students in your ESL night classes?"

"Yes, there are several Vietnamese students, ranging in age from 25 to 75. Why do you ask?"

"Because it appears that some of our students don't even know there are Vietnamese people living among us. Or that their classmates may be Vietnamese, not Chinese. Or have any appreciation for what these people have sacrificed to come to this country."

There was silence until Mr. Picket spoke again, his face crumpled. "I am personally mortified by the incident that occurred yesterday. And I need your help, all of your help, in finding ways to educate our students about the importance of diversity and the richness of our country as a result of immigrants leaving their homes to settle here." He paused, drew in a deep breath and continued.

"I have an assignment for our next meeting. I'd like each of you to contribute an idea about how we can combat intolerance in our school. We'll start next week's meeting an hour earlier. Thank you for coming today."

I spoke up: "What action are you taking about the boys who bullied Tran yesterday?"

He responded: "I've contacted their parents about meeting with me along with their sons on Wednesday evening. I'd like you to attend this meeting, Miss O'Neil, if you can arrange it."

"Of course," I replied, already dreading the confrontation and defensive attitudes I knew we'd encounter. "Shall we meet tomorrow to prepare?"

"Certainly," Mr. Picket said as he closed the meeting. I thought he looked older than his 50 years.

I was gathering my things when Mr. Picket tapped me lightly on my arm. "Callie, will you stay for a moment?" I was Callie when others weren't around, and he was Tom. I had worked for him for eight years and respected his commitment to education and to the students. We had never had a serious disagreement.

"Sure, Tom," I responded.

"I think we should invite Tran's parents to meet separately with us. Do you agree?" Tom's tone was still grave.

"Yes, we owe them an apology at least. Were you planning to have Tran there as well?" Tom inhaled, then looked directly at me. His caterpillar gray eyebrows met in a V as he considered my question. "Yes, I guess so. We're asking the culprits to come with their parents, so we should be consistent with Tran."

"I agree."

"Callie, I'm sorry to drag you into this ugly situation, but you were the unfortunate faculty member who discovered the boy. I know you have a full schedule with your evening language classes. But I think your ESL experience will be very valuable in dealing with Tran."

"I'm happy to help." I quickly reconsidered my response. "Maybe, 'happy' isn't the right word. I'm willing to help. To tell you the truth, I'm not looking forward to the meetings. Either one of them."

He shook his head slightly, "Neither am I. In fact, I'm dreading them. But we have no choice, do we?" Tom turned toward the door. I didn't need to answer his last question and followed him out. I wondered if I looked older than my 40 years. I certainly felt it today.

*****

Three evenings later, my temples throbbed with nerves as the parents and their sons shuffled into the conference room. Everyone appeared subdued. The Nelsons, Mr. Jones without his wife, the Gilespis, Buddy Hall's parents, and Mrs. Shaw.

Mr. Jones looked particularly surly. He limped badly, so I gave him the benefit of the doubt. Perhaps he'd injured his leg and was in pain.

No one said anything as they seated themselves, but the room hummed with tension. The boys occasionally smirked when they caught each other's eyes. Reproving looks from their parents ended their acting up. Rather than chatting to each other, the adults examined their shoes or the institutional safety posters on the walls.

Mr. Picket greeted the group solemnly and introduced me as the faculty member who had found Tran bleeding on the floor and also as an ESL expert. A few mothers offered me weak, embarrassed smiles. I returned their looks with what I hoped was a gracious nod. The fathers continued their examination of the floor.

The parents were dressed in "respectful" outfits, and the boys looked better than usual. No butts showing. Buddy clutched his skate board, as he always did. I wondered if he slept with it, like a favorite pet.

Mr. Picket asked the boys why they had attacked Tran. Their explanations were extraordinarily righteous and delivered without the slightest hint of remorse. Tran's food stunk. He had no right to eat at "their" table. He didn't belong to their group, etc. They didn't come right out and say Tran was Asian, but the implication was loud and clear. They obviously thought their actions were completely justified.

Mr. Picket then opened the discussion to parents' remarks. The parents divided between defending their sons out of family loyalty or embarrassed comments about the racial overtones to the incident. I wondered if anyone would step up to a discussion about the boys' using violence to express their feelings. When no one did, I asked the question, and was met by silence. Mr. Picket sent me a grateful look.

Mr. Jones finally spoke up. With his chin jutting forward and his face flushing, he shouted, "My son is an American. He don't need to apologize for attacking some gook who should stay in his own country anyhow."

Stunned silence. Mrs. Shaw cleared her throat. "I don't agree with you. What our sons did was shameful and un-American. That boy was innocent."

Mr. Jones slammed out of the room, dragging his bad leg. His final words were, "You don't know nothin' about being an American." His son, Tim, remained in his seat, blushing right up to the tips of his ears. I had a feeling his father's performance was predictable.

The outcome of the meeting was detention for the boys. Not one boy claimed innocence, so each of the culprits had classroom and school grounds clean up duty for one month. After the punishment was discussed, Mr. Picket addressed the boys:

"The cafeteria belongs to the school district, as do the tables and chairs. You may sit anywhere you please, but that is also true for other students. You do not own a table simply because you and your friends typically eat there. Do you understand?" No response.

His voice became louder and more confrontational: "Let me ask again, do you understand that you have no right to exclude anyone from eating at any table?" Parents elbowed their sons sharply until the boys nodded, eyes averted. Another "no win," I thought.

One of the mothers suggested that each boy write an apology letter to Tran. From the look on the boys' faces, I surmised that the mothers would probably do the writing, coercing their sons to sign the letters.

I didn't think this was an effective solution, so I spoke up: "Racial conflict often happens when someone unfamiliar comes into a classroom, someone from a different culture, someone who looks different. In this case, someone who eats food that smells different from your sons'. I think that education might be a better, long term solution. Do you agree?"

Some parents looked perplexed; others nodded. The boys looked bored. Mr. Picket nodded vigorously. "Mr. Picket and I will discuss an education plan with the faculty and notify you about the activities we'd like your boys to participate in. The more we know about a different culture, the more we accept it. Do we have your concurrence?"

Buddy, the leader of the culprits, said in a stage whisper, "Does that include Hitler? He was different."

Mr. Picket immediately jumped in, "Buddy, we are not referring to evil. We're talking about your appreciating the values of other nationalities and all our ancestors who made the US the great country it is today." Buddy looked unconvinced. His mother placed her hand on his thigh to stop him from kicking the chair in front of him.

Mr. Picket asked: "Are any of you descendants of Native Americans?" No one raised a hand. "That means that everyone in this room has roots in another country, maybe from a very different culture, and probably another language. Can you picture your grandfather or great-grandfather being attacked because the sausage in his lunch bag smelled? Or your grandmother because her clothes weren't from the Gap?" No response.

Mrs. Shaw broke the awkward silence. "I think that an education plan is heading us in the right direction." The Gilespis and the Nelsons also signaled "yes." The others remained impassive. They were the loyal-till-death parents. Who knew what to expect from them.

Mr. Picket thanked the parents for coming and promised to send them an education plan within two weeks. He reiterated that the boys were compelled to participate in the plan as part of their punishment. Did everyone understand that? Did the boys understand that? Nods all around. The boys shuffled out behind their parents, reminding me of the field workers in North Carolina who seemed to have all the time in the world to walk home after grueling, long days in the tobacco fields. What had these boys done to exhibit such fatigue?

Tom and I were exhausted. "Well, Callie, how did we do?" he asked as we rearranged the circle of chairs.

"I wish I knew. I think the education plan is an excellent idea. If only I had the energy to start drafting it tonight."

He reassured me. "Let's see what the faculty comes up with for their educational diversity assignment."

We turned off the lights and went our separate ways.

Chapter 3

Tran

At lunch the following day, I casually entered the cafeteria at lunchtime. Buddy's gang were at their usual table. There was no sign of Tran. I checked the gym and several classrooms. Finally, I wandered outside to the quad and spotted him sitting on the ground by himself in a corner, his back against the wall. His head was bowed, and his food untouched.

Well, I said to myself, you've found him. What's next? I walked slowly in his direction, clearing my throat to avoid startling him. He glanced up at me, then immediately down at his knees.

"Tran, I'm so sorry about what happened yesterday. I haven't had a chance to tell you that."

He murmured, "It's Okay."

"Has Buddy's group bullied you before?"

"Not exactly," he answered evasively.

"Would you like to talk about it?"

"No. I mean, no thank you."

I smiled at his good manners. "Tran, I don't know if you are aware that I teach English to foreign adults at night."

"I heard Mr. Picket say that last night."

"I know how difficult it can be for immigrants to fit into new cultures. I wish that weren't the case, but it certainly is a reality." No comment and no eye contact from Tran.

"Tran, will you tell me about your family?"

He hesitated, then looked straight at me for the first time. "My mother is still in Saigon. My father was an officer in the Republican Army and is in a re-education camp. I live with my cousins who escaped as boat people."

I drew in a sharp breath. This boy was practically an orphan. His English was fluid and colloquial, but the pain that seeped between his words was palpable.

"You are a brave young man to be living here without your parents." He didn't respond, so I asked, "Will your cousins be coming to the meeting with Mr. Picket tomorrow night?"

"Yes."

"Do they speak English?"

"Yes, they've taken ESL classes."

"Well, I'm looking forward to meeting them. Please tell them that."

"I will." Tran ended the conversation by taking the first bite of a piece of fruit I'd never seen before. I turned away and walked straight to Tom's office. We had some thinking to do before tomorrow afternoon's meeting.

****

Tom and I didn't have much of an agenda for the meeting with Tran and his cousins, aside from apologizing and describing our vague thoughts about an education plan for the school.

The following afternoon, we were both nervous and quiet as we watched the institutional clock on Tom's office wall inch toward 4:00.

At exactly the appointed hour, we heard a timid knock on Tom's door. We both stood and converted our worried expressions to professional smiles that didn't reach our eyes. Tran preceded Tony who was dressed neatly in chinos and an immaculate white button-down shirt, sleeves rolled up to his elbows. His black hair was neatly cut, a perfectly straight part displaying his tan scalp. He was slender, with sinewy hairless forearms. Altogether an attractive middle-aged man.

Thu followed respectfully behind her brother. She looked frail and wore a drab blouse hanging loosely over tan slacks. The clothes overpowered her tiny frame. Her black hair was carefully tied in a low bun, held fast with a spangled hair clip. Her face was neutral and indistinguishable from other Asian women I'd met. She seemed very uncomfortable.

Tran also seemed nervous. He was a small boy, compared to Americans of his age, slender, but wiry and good looking. The men didn't look alike, but shared an aura of quiet confidence, unlike Thu who clasped and unclasped her fingers.

Tom held out his hand as he introduced himself and me. Tony shook it firmly and introduced his sister, who clasped her hands behind her. No hand shaking for her. She bowed her head in greeting and avoided eye contact with Tom and me. I experienced a sinking feeling in my stomach, guessing this was not going to be easy.

They politely refused offers of coffee, tea or water and stiffly sat on the edges of their chairs around Tom's round guest table. Tran sat between his cousins, his eyes darting from Tom to Tony. He never even glanced at me.

Tom began: "Thank you so much for coming." Tony and Thu regarded him neutrally without responding. "Let me begin by apologizing for the boys' behavior to Tran. As far as we know, Tran did nothing to provoke the boys' actions."

Thu looked blank when Tom used the word "provoke." I tried to help.

"Tran did nothing wrong. The boys just didn't want him to sit at a table they think is theirs." Thu's frown disappeared, and her face resumed its neutral expression. I hoped she was reassured that Tran was an innocent victim.

Tom continued: "We have met with the boys and their parents and explained that their behavior was unacceptable and that the boys will be punished."

Tran's eyes widened in fright. I guessed he was worried about retaliation. The room was quiet, but the cloud over the Vietnamese family darkened.

Tony finally spoke up. "I told Tran to sit at the boys' table. I thought they would accept him after a while. I was wrong." Tran stared at his knees. Thu continued to examine her clenched hands.

I couldn't bear it any longer. The ESL teacher in me took over. "Tony and Thu, please let me try to explain the situation. There are very few Asians at our school and not many in our town, as you must know. When children see someone who looks different and eats different food, they are often unkind. Some adults have the same reaction. Their behavior shows they are ignorant. Do you understand what I'm saying?"

Thu looked at me for the first time, and Tony nodded and said: "We are familiar with ignorance. It is not just children who are unfriendly to us. We experience it every day."

Tony saw my embarrassment and continued, "Miss O'Neil, we come from Vietnam where we were treated like dirt under the communist government. Unfriendly children cannot hurt us."

Tom and I looked mortified. Land of the free slid out of my heart. After a moment, Tom cleared his throat and offered: "Miss O'Neil and I are educators. We take our jobs seriously and will do everything in our power to help our students understand that this country ensures that everyone is treated equally."

For the first time, Tran spoke. His voice was firm and low: "I am an American. I know what the Constitution says. If the boys don't accept me, that's Okay. But it won't change my life. When I finish school, I'm going to be a doctor or an engineer. I'm going to drive a fast car and live in a big house with my cousins."

The adults were stunned by this brave statement. I couldn't hold back a huge smile. "Good for you, Tran. I'm sure you will follow your dreams." I wanted to hug him, but knew this wasn't appropriate.

Tran's declaration seemed to end the conference. As we all stood up, Tom reassured our guests that the faculty would be monitoring the bullies and that they would be punished. Tran's parting comment was, "Don't worry, I'm going to take karate. What happened last week won't happen again." And he walked out with his chin up, followed by his cousins. I believed him.

Chapter 4

Cam's Story

My adult advanced ELW (English Language Writing) class met that night. There were eight students: two from Vietnam, one from Taiwan, three from Central America, and one from Jordan. I hated to admit to myself that my favorites by far were the two Vietnamese women, both boat people. Cam was extroverted, funny and wise. She was married and had two children.

Lien was lovely, shy and serious. Her husband, an officer in the South Vietnamese Army, had been captured and interred by the victorious communist army.

A month before, I had instructed my students to write an essay about their life, any incident that was important to them, or about someone who had influenced them, or a memory that simply will stay with them forever. They had been drafting paragraphs for the previous two months, but this was their first long piece. I was really looking forward to reading them.

After several discussions and many drafts, Cam completed her essay.

Cam's Story – The Tet Offensive

New Year's Day, 1968. I was 18. I had shopped for a new dress and matching high heeled shoes. I had cut out a page from a fashion magazine showing a beautiful model with a complicated hair style – tiny braids in the front, gathered somehow in the back, fastened with a velvet ribbon. I had pinned the page to my bedroom wall several days before and planned to fix my hair exactly like it for New Years.

New Years in Vietnam means three days of no school, no housework, only fun. My friends and I planned to start the holiday by going to a movie, then meeting more friends at our favorite restaurant.

While I was putting on my new outfit, I heard the sound of firecrackers nearby. This was typical of our Vietnamese New Year celebration.

My sister and I left the house, dressed in our best, heading for the bridge where we'd meet our friends on the way to the movie. The magazine hairdo had proved too difficult, but I thought the French braid I'd managed looked good.

Two blocks from the meeting place, we slowed our pace the moment we saw a group of men in red and khaki uniforms on the bridge about 50 feet away from us. Red Army soldiers – what were they doing here? We lived in Hue, a small town East of Saigon. Hue was not an army post.

My sister and I needed only a glance to communicate our panic about what the soldiers might do if they saw us. Calmly and slowly we turned around and headed for home. Both of us wanted to remove our high heels and run, but knew that attracting attention was a bad idea. We were dripping with sweat when we arrived home safely.

The year before a new family had moved to Hue. My father was always gracious to newcomers and went out of his way to welcome them. The family set up an alternations/seamstress shop, and my parents took our small mending jobs to them early on, helping them to grow their business.

A few days after the Tet Offensive, I recognized the father of the family dressed smartly in a Red Army officer's uniform. When I told my parents this astounding news, my father explained that the family were probably spies, sent ahead to learn about our city in preparation for the communist take-over. "Communists are very patient people," my father explained.

The Red Army began arresting dissidents soon after New Year's Day. Our family was petrified my father would be taken since he had served in the South Vietnamese army. He had retired and gone to work doing odd jobs at a university lab, but he clearly had a military background, and therefore, was a potential threat to the communists.

Six months after the Offensive, two men dressed completely in black, came to our house late one night and took him away. My mother and all of us children cried because we thought we'd never see him again.

To our amazement and joy, he returned a week later. When we asked what had happened during his time away, he replied simply that the soldiers asked a lot of questions. That's all he would say. In retrospect, I wonder if his kindness to the seamstress family earned his release. We'll never know.

There had always been a cold war between the Catholics and the Buddhists in Hue. The Catholics were extremely powerful in our town because of their close relationship with the government.

In the mid-1960s we had been forced to sell our home because the Catholics intended to build a new church on our block. Our neighbors on either side were also forced to move. My father said we had no choice, no legal recourse, once the government made a decision. We moved to a house not far from the old one.

Construction on the new church had not begun yet when the communists took over, but our old house and our neighbors' had been demolished. All that was left was a large vacant lot.

In January 1968, the communists rounded up about 2,000 people who had worked for the South Vietnamese government and herded them to our old land. They instructed the prisoners to dig a shallow trench. When it was completed, they tied the prisoners together, lined them up in front of the trench and shot them so that their bodies fell into the trench.

We could hear the shots from our house. I wanted to find out what was happening, but my father told me to stay inside with the others while he investigated. He returned several minutes later, white-faced and nauseated. He told us about the bodies lying in the shallow grave, barely covered with dirt. Some of them were still alive.

"I want to see it for myself," I declared.

My father responded, "You don't want to see what I just saw. You'll never forget it. The sight will haunt you the rest of your life."

"I don't care. I want to see for myself." And I did. My father was right. I'll never forget it.

Chapter 5

Karate and a Party

About a month later, just before Spring break, I was in the faculty break room when the school nurse, Tavena, came in, shaking her head. "What's wrong?" I asked.

"You won't believe what just happened! Buddy came in my office, blubbering like a baby, cradling his arm. There was a big bruise on his thigh, too."

"What happened to him? Is there a new bigger bully in school?" I asked.

Tavena grinned broadly, "No, there's a new karate champ, it seems. Tran's been taking lessons and defended himself when Buddy tried to shove him into his locker. I wish I could have seen it."

All eight teachers in the faculty room began to clap. I contributed the wolf whistle my father taught me as a teenager.

*****

Tran couldn't keep the triumphant smile off his face when he arrived home that day. Thu was in the kitchen as usual. "Hungry?" she asked as she did every day.

"Starving," Tran answered.

"Why you so happy?" Boa asked, smiling back at him.

"I'll tell you when Tony gets home. What's there to eat?"

Two hours later, Tony, Boa and Tran sat together for dinner. Thu addressed her brother, "Tran has good news to tell us."

Tony's face was typically neutral as he turned to his cousin, "What happened today, Tran?"

Tran tried to mimic his cousin's neutral expression but couldn't stifle his excitement. "Buddy, the same boy that threw me against the wall, tried to stuff me into my locker after lunch. I used a karate chop to his arm and landed a perfect kick on his leg. He cried like a baby. His friends just stood there and watched Buddy stumble and fall. I think his nose was bleeding." Tran looked triumphant.

Tony and Thu exchanged a worried look. Tony asked, "Will that mean you will be in trouble with Mr. Picket?"

"I don't think so. Buddy already went to the nurse, and I'm sure she told the principal what happened. No one called me out of class this afternoon."

Tony and Thu sighed in relief, then turned to Tran. "Your father would be proud of you. And I'm proud of you," Tony said.

Tran smiled and thanked him. "I know the karate lessons are expensive. I'll pay you back as soon as I get a job."

Tony assured him, "No worries. You are not a big boy and need to protect yourself from bad boys. I'm happy you used what you learned." As an afterthought, Tony added, "Maybe you'll teach me?"

Tran laughed, "Are you afraid someone will stuff you in your locker at the plant?"

Tony smiled, "They haven't tried yet. I'm the supervisor." And Thu joined in their moment of happiness.

*****

Cam clapped in delight when I returned her essay with a huge A at the top. Her eyes were dancing, and she thanked me with a birthday-girl smile. I gave her a quick hug and said she certainly deserved an A.

The following week after class, Cam bowed slightly as she handed me an envelope decorated with a small dragon. "Shall I open it now?" I asked her.

"As you please," she answered. I remembered my lack of understanding of polite phrases when working in

London. When British people answer your question with "I don't mind," they really mean I don't agree with you at all, which I learned the hard way, thinking my co-workers thought my suggestions were wonderful. I wondered if "as you please" was also a trap for American English speakers, so I thanked Cam and tucked the envelope into my purse.

I opened it when I arrived home that night and was delighted to find an invitation to a party to celebrate Cam's A. On the following Saturday night, I was to go to Cam's home at 6:00 p.m. There was no RSVP, but I quickly wrote an acceptance note, thinking Cam would want to know I was coming. I pasted a tiny American flag on the corner of the envelope and mailed it the following morning.

The rest of the school week was uneventful except for one remarkable incident. I went searching for Tran at lunch time the next day, but didn't see him in the quad, nor the classrooms. The last place I looked was the cafeteria, because I knew he avoided it. I decided to pretend I was looking for another faculty member and quickly scanned the tables. There he was at the bullies' table, calmly eating noodles, while Buddy's boys punched each other's shoulders and laughed loudly at jokes I thankfully couldn't hear. But the spectacle of Tran sitting quietly in the center of the enemy amazed me. What had happened?

I found the answer in history class that afternoon. Carley, the sprinter, was telling two girlfriends about Buddy's new bodyguard. In her high, giggly voice,

Carley gushed that Buddy had appointed Tran to be his bodyguard since he was now a karate expert. It appeared that Tran had accepted the position. I did what my sister and I had done for years around our parents – sucked in my cheeks to keep from laughing. Cheers for Tran!

*****

On the Saturday night of Cam's party, I debated how to dress. Should I be the demure teacher in a denim skirt, simple blouse and sensible shoes? Or should I let the woman inside come out, the way I used to be before the divorce? I surprised myself by choosing my red dress with the scooped neck and dangling silver earrings. They showed off better when my hair was pulled up, so I created a semi-chignon and fastened it with a sparkly clip that complemented my auburn hair. When I stepped into my high strappy sandals I noticed the skirt was shorter than I remembered. I shrugged and grabbed a clutch bag and headed for the door.

As I drove into Cam's neighborhood, I noticed that the shop signs were in both English and Asian characters. The houses were small with tidy front yards, interspersed with older three-story apartment buildings that needed make-overs.

I found a parking spot three houses away from Cam's bungalow. I could hear music, laughter and Vietnamese conversation. As soon as I knocked on the door, Cam threw it open and beamed at me. "I'm so happy you came, Miss O'Neil." She was wearing a beautiful pink silk shirt over new-looking jeans. Her hair was piled on her head, making her look far more sophisticated than her appearance at night school.

I returned her greeting: "I'm so happy you invited me."

As I followed Cam into the entry-way, then into the living room, the guests' conversations seemed to falter as they turned to look at me. Was it the red dress? I quickly scanned the other women and saw with relief that they too had dressed up.

So it wasn't my outfit. It apparently was that I was the only non-Asian at the party. I was very comfortable being a minority. Because of my ESL classes, I knew the best plan was to smile and quietly speak to Cam's family and be introduced to their friends, one-by-one. I didn't speak Vietnamese, but guessed that these people spoke English.

Cam proudly introduced me to her elderly parents, to her husband and then to the other guests. As I surmised, everyone switched to English when I approached.

Cam excused herself to open the door each time a new guest arrived. Otherwise, she remained at my side.

I glanced at the newest arrivals and was surprised to see Tran, Tony and Thu in the entry. Tran smiled shyly at me. Tony and Thu inclined their heads slightly, respectfully. Thu was lovely in a green and coral silk dress that flowed over her tiny frame. Her ponytail was fastened with a matching coral scarf. Tony had a "just out of the shower" look with comb marks in his hair. He looked very American in nice-fitting jeans and a freshly ironed white button-down shirt. Sister and brother were very attractive.

As Cam began to make introductions, I put my hand on her arm and said, "Cam, I have met Tran and his cousins. We don't need introductions." And I smiled at them. "Tran is a student at Acacia, where I teach during the day."

Cam replied, "I thought you might have taught Tony and Thu in your night classes."

"No, I haven't had that pleasure," I said. Tony smiled warmly, and Thu shyly averted her eyes.

I was surprised when Tran explained that they were all cousins. I simply didn't expect Cam and Tran to be related, but why not?

Our conversation was interrupted by Cam's elderly father who clapped to get everyone's attention. He raised a glass in Cam's direction and spoke in Vietnamese. Cam blushed and smiled, and everyone toasted her. Tony joined me and without being asked, translated, "This party is to celebrate my daughter's high achievement in English writing. She received an A on her writing story. We are very proud of her." Everyone applauded.

Cam responded first in Vietnamese then in accented, perfect English: "Thank you, Father. Thank you to everyone who came to my party. I feel proud today. I feel proud to be an American. My English teacher, Miss

O'Neil, is here tonight. I want to thank her for helping me and coming to my party." I smiled as everyone clapped.

The loudest clapping came from children, whom I guessed were Cam's. Her husband Binh was keeping a close eye on them, I supposed to ensure they behaved themselves.

When the speeches were over, Tony and I talked quietly. I asked him about his job, and he asked me how I managed teaching both day and night. I didn't tell him that since my divorce, I filled the lonely evening hours correcting papers and creating lesson plans. Instead, I told him part of the truth. "I love teaching English to adults, but it doesn't pay enough, so I teach at Acacia to earn a living."

He asked, "If you could earn enough teaching adults, would you leave your job at Acacia?"

I surprised myself with how quickly I responded, "In a heartbeat." His brows furrowed, and I realized I'd used slang Tony didn't understand. "I mean, absolutely yes."

He nodded and said, "Then you should find a way to do what you love. That's the best part of being in American. You can follow your dream." I looked at him in awe.

After a minute, I told him, "I learn more from my students than they do from me. That's why I love teaching adults." Tony grinned, understanding that he had become my teacher for the moment.

We were interrupted by Cam's mother, a tiny, wizened woman with a wire coat hanger head and neck and nearly bald head bent over her cane. She raised her black eyes to us and spoke in Vietnamese. Tony translated. "Where are your children?"

I was astounded by her question and blushed as I answered, "I don't have children, I'm sorry to say."

She continued, "Where is your husband?" Tony averted his eyes as he asked these direct, personal questions.

"I am divorced."

One more arrow came from the old woman's mouth, "Why don't you find another husband?" Her shriveled hand trembled on the cane.

"Well, I haven't been looking for one." The old woman squinted her rheumy eyes, but made direct contact with mine.

"You need to find a good man before you get old. You don't want to marry an old man." I laughed and told her she was right about that. I could feel Tony's discomfort. He placed his hand under my elbow and spoke in Vietnamese to the old woman, I assumed excusing us.

He guided me toward the dining room and gave me a verbal tour of the many bowls and trays of food. Nothing more was said about my single status.

I had enjoyed Pho, a delicious, spicy soup, at a Vietnamese restaurant that Acacia teachers went to occasionally for lunch, but was out of my depth with the display in front of me. Tony suggested I take a taste of each dish and began selecting samples for my plate, describing the contents of each. My plate was embarrassingly full. "How about you? Are you hungry?"

"I'll join you in a minute. I'll see if my sister needs anything."

I looked around for a place to sit with my overloaded plate and spotted a chair in the living room. Tony found me and squatted next to my chair, his plate about half as full as mine. "You aren't eating much," I noticed.

"I try to eat small meals several times a day, just the way we do in Vietnam."

"That's probably a lot healthier than the way Americans eat," I commented.

"I agree," Tony said, "but I don't think that food in this country is important. Being free is more important."

I wasn't sure I understood what he was trying to say, but decided not to pursue the subject. A party was not the right venue for this conversation.

Cam approached, holding the hands of two children. "I would like you to meet my children, Miss O'Neil. This is Tamara and this is Leon."

I offered my hand to each solemn child and said, "I'm very happy to meet both of you. Your mother has told me what wonderful children you are." Both serious looks melted into delighted smiles. They looked up at their mother who returned their grins, then back at me.

47

Leon asked, "Are you our mommy's teacher?"

"Yes, I am."

"Is she always good in class?"

I stifled a laugh and answered seriously, avoiding eye contact with Cam, "Yes, your mother is always well behaved. She does all her homework on time. She is very smart."

Tamara dropped her mother's hand and twirled around, singing, "Mommy is a smart girl. Mommy is a good girl."

"That's enough," Cam said, but there was no sternness in her voice or her face. She hugged her children and sent them to bed. "I'll be there in a minute."

I told her, "Cam, your children are beautiful." Her eyes teared, and she murmured a simple thank you.

On the drive home from the party, I found myself humming and feeling happy. I couldn't remember the last time I felt this way.

Chapter 6

Lien's Story

Because Cam was so open and friendly, I found myself wondering about Lien, my other Vietnamese student in the advanced writing class. She often looked exhausted when she arrived at school. But she was never too tired to ask excellent questions about our difficult language. For example, she asked me to explain the difference between 'a' white house and 'the' white house – which led to a conversation about a yellow jacket, the bee, and a yellow jacket that you wore. Oh my, English is challenging.

Lien submitted her essay a week late. She apologized and explained that an American friend had helped her edit it, so that was why she was late. I patted her hand and told her I knew how hard she worked and how much I was looking forward to reading her essay. Her tense shoulders relaxed as she smiled a shy thank you.

Lien's Story

I met my husband, Van, at a party celebrating a big battle victory for the South Vietnamese army. He was a war hero that night and charmed me and my friends. Our meeting was brief because he was transferred to Saigon the week after the party. I didn't see him for another year.

In the meantime, I met and fell in love with a local young man and wanted to marry him. It was a bad idea. He turned out to be a ladies' man. While he swore he loved only me, he supposedly got another girl pregnant. His family forced him to marry her. The girl apparently only thought she was pregnant. There was no baby. But he had already married her, and my heart was broken.

A year later, I was on vacation in Saigon with a girl friend. We went to a nightclub to hear a popular singing group. Who should be hanging out with the singers but Van! We recognized each other immediately. He was very friendly and introduced me and my friend to the singers. We were thrilled.

Van offered to give us a tour of the city the following day. We readily accepted. He was a charming and knowledgeable tour guide, and he paid for everything. It was a great day.

A week later, Van called to say he had been transferred to my city and could we see each other. I was delighted. My father wasn't. "The best way to become a widow is to marry a military man." My mother objected to Van being much older than I was. I didn't object to anything about him. I was attracted to his maturity and handsome face.

My father always wanted the best for me. He wanted me to study, and I got a job instead. He wanted me to marry a wealthy farmer, and I wanted to marry a soldier. My father wanted me to learn to cook and sew, and I wanted to dress up and go to parties. He couldn't stop me from going out but was always waiting up for me to get home, regardless of the hour.

Many years later, my siblings told me how my father took out his frustrations with me on them and on my mother. He could never control me, but we loved each other deeply.

I was always popular in school. Boys used to give my sister notes to deliver to me with money tucked into their envelopes. My sister told me that she kept the money and tore up the notes.

I dated Van for a year before he proposed to me, and I accepted. When he walked up the path to our house, my father would escape to a room at the back. As a last resort, Van brought his general to our house to convince my father to give his permission for the marriage. "Van is an upstanding, honest, loyal man. He will make a fine husband." My father was never convinced.

One night Van took me to a club where his ex-girlfriend was the lead singer. After the performance we were having a drink at a table outside. Van's body guards were with us, as always. As I sipped my drink, I heard some commotion behind me. As I turned to look, one of the body guards ran forward, picked me up and carried me to the waiting car. I glanced over his shoulder to see the second body guard restraining the singer who was clutching a champagne bottle intended to crush my head. It seemed that Van had more than one girlfriend. Hopefully, the others were not so jealous and dangerous.

My father finally agreed, and Van and I were married in 1971. Marriage in Vietnam is not as formal as in America. If a man and woman live together and have a child, they are considered to be married. Van's first wife lived in the North. She had told him she was pregnant, so he dutifully married her. When the baby grew a little older, he looked nothing like Van or his family. Van suspected he had been tricked.

When I realized I was pregnant, Van asked his wife for a divorce. She refused and said there wasn't enough money in the world for him to buy his freedom. She enjoyed being the wife of an officer and using his highly respected family name. Later, I found out that she had paid a voodoo witch to weave a spell that would kill me. She was very jealous, although she and Van led completely separate lives. When Van visited her to ask for a divorce, he met her children conceived by other men.

There was further trouble from her that nearly caused Van to be demoted. She had purchased a villa in her husband's name and didn't pay the mortgage. The government came after Van to pay the debt, which he did, then sold the property.

As I wrote a huge A on her essay, I thanked heaven for my job. Where else would I hear heroic stories like Lien's? As I re-read the story, I realized how angry Lien still was with her husband's first wife after more than twenty years.

And I wondered what happened to her husband.

Chapter 7

Tran and Callie

Tran was completely taken aback seeing Miss O'Neil at Cam's party. He couldn't believe how pretty she looked in her red dress, with her auburn hair in an elegant upsweep.

He was further amazed to see his cousin Tony's appreciative expression when he looked at Miss O'Neil. He watched as Tony translated whatever Cam's mother was saying to her and guessed her comments were rude, as he had experienced himself. "Do you have a girlfriend yet?" she had asked him, thumping his head with her tiny fist. When he shook his head, she said, "Why not? You not that ugly."

He noticed that Tony had remained attentive to Miss O'Neil throughout the party. Tony had never had a girlfriend, at least since Tran had lived with his cousins. Tran had never asked either Tony or Thu about their personal relationships, just as they never asked him about his. Their mutual respect was precious to Tran. He knew he would never mention Miss O'Neil outside of a conversation about school business. He wondered if American families had similar unspoken rules.

The week after Cam's party, Miss O'Neil stopped him in the corridor to ask how he was doing. He ducked his head and muttered "fine." She paused, apparently waiting for him to look at her, which he eventually did. "Would you like to talk to me about anything, Tran?" Her voice was gentle and caring. He hesitated.

"Yes, I would." He surprised himself with his answer.

"How about in the gym right after school? We can talk while the kids are playing basketball."

"Okay."

Tran's mind started to churn. What would they talk about? Could he ask her how to get Hanna to notice him? Could he tell her about missing his mother? About his nightmares of what could be happening to his father? Would it be Okay to ask how she felt about Tony?

He had no idea how to talk to an American woman, a teacher who didn't even teach any of his classes. After the initial panic, he felt himself relaxing. What did he have to lose, as Buddy's friends asked each other constantly. He felt his nervousness melt into anticipation and even excitement as the day progressed.

At 3:05 Tran tentatively poked his head into the gym. The noise from the basketballs was deafening. He spotted Miss O'Neil sitting on the highest row of the bleachers. He slowly climbed up to join her.

"Hi Tran. I think the basketball noise will drown out our conversation. I'm very happy we have a chance to talk."

"Me, too," Tran added shyly. His unsettled dark eyes flitted from the game below to her face.

She kept her voice low, under the sound of the slamming balls, so he had to lean toward her to hear. "I saw you sitting at Buddy's table in the cafeteria. How in the world did that happen? The last time you did that, I found you bleeding on the floor."

"I've been taking karate lessons. Ever since Buddy tried to shove me in my locker and I landed a couple of good karate shots on him, I've become his bodyguard." Tran couldn't suppress a smile.

Callie returned the smile and swung her legs around to face Tran. "Tran, tell me about living in Illinois. Are you happy here?"

Tran looked thoughtful before he answered. "I am lucky to be in America."

"But I asked if you were happy."

Tran hesitated and finally spoke thoughtfully. "It's complicated. My cousins are wonderful to me. But I miss my family in Vietnam, and my friends, and the river." Callie sensed he had much more to say, so she remained quiet to give him time.

His eyes looked anguished, "It's my dad I worry most about. My mom has heard nothing from him in a long time."

"Where is he exactly?"

"In a re-education camp in Hanoi. That means he's in prison, probably doing hard labor, like on a chain gang breaking up stones for paving roads."

"Can he write to you?"

"No, the only way my mom gets news is from prison guards or prisoners who have been released."

"Is there a chance he'll be released?"

"Not really. He was an officer in the South Vietnamese Army. All the officers were either shot or sentenced to life in prison. He could be dead, but my mom and I heard a story that gives us a little hope."

"I'd like to hear about it if you feel like telling me. I promise not to discuss it with anyone."

Tran looked directly at her, breathed deeply, then began. "When the Red Army invaded my dad's post, they rounded up all the officers. My dad was hiding in a supply building where several soldiers from our side had been shot. He stripped one of the fallen men and changed into the enlisted man's uniform, dressing the dead man in his officer's uniform."

Tran continued in a deliberately neutral voice: "When my dad was captured within hours, he was pushed into a truck with other soldiers. The following week, there was a mock trial where everyone was convicted and sentenced to prison for life. My dad was lucky he wasn't shot like all the officers." Tran bowed his head. Callie reached over and laid her hand gently on his shoulder. He didn't pull away.

"I'm so sorry, Tran. Not knowing if your father is dead or alive must be torture for you and your mother."

"As long as we don't hear he is dead, we have hope." But his voice was full of despair.

"How did you get to the United States? And why did your mother stay in Vietnam?"

Tran's sad face transformed into a teasing grin. "I will give you a copy of the English essay I wrote last year. It will explain everything."

"Perfect! I can't wait to read it. Please put it in my cubby in the teachers' lounge."

"Okay, tomorrow."

"Good. I'll look for it." Callie paused, "Tran, I asked if you wanted to talk to me about anything and all you've done today is answer my questions. That's my fault. I really am interested in hearing what's on your mind and in your heart. Is there something special you want to talk about?"

He thought for a moment. "Yes, there are several things I'd like to talk to you about." Then the teasing smile returned, "but you've used up all our time. I have to get home to do my homework. My cousin will worry if I'm late."

"I'm sorry. How about another meeting? I promise not to hog the conversation. Next week? Same time, same place?"

"Deal," Tran grinned and raised his hand for a high-five.

*****

Tran's Essay

I grew up in the Delta in a house built on stilts because of the annual floods. We kids loved flood time because we could fish right off the front porch. We took a sampan to school.

My father was in the Special Forces. He went away to war in 1975, leaving my mother with three kids. My mother got a job at the embassy in Saigon. We lived with our grandparents, and my mother came home on weekends. My grandfather was a doctor.

On April 18, my mother was able to get four tickets to leave Vietnam. Because there was martial law which meant that soldiers shot anyone on the streets after 5:30 p.m., four of us piled on a motor bike heading for a sugar cane field to hide until nightfall. I still have a scar on my left calf from the motor bike burn. When the sun set, a taxi came to take us to the airport.

In Vietnam, a family consists of parents and children, but also includes grandparents. My mother felt guilty about leaving them behind. At the airport, I read my book and stayed in the waiting area right where my mother told me to wait.

Sometime later when I heard the other passengers begin to gather their things, I realized my mom and four-

59

year-old-sister were gone. So was my brother. She had left and taken my siblings to get paperwork for my grandparents to join us. The people around me in the waiting room pulled me into the line, and I boarded the plane. My mother and my siblings missed the plane.

I wore a sign around my neck with my name printed on it. That's all I had. I flew to Guam, then the Philippines, and eventually to Camp Pendleton in California. My great aunt lived in Pasadena, so U.S. immigration officers contacted her, and she agreed to sponsor me. I was seven.

My aunt worked for Pacific Bell. I lived with her for 2 years. She was a spinster and a strict Catholic. Her first words to me were "You will never speak a word of Vietnamese in my house." She reared me in the "old school" way. I spent many hours inside the dark cold marble walls of Saint Andrews Church. When I was home, I spent many lonely hours in my bedroom crying.

At a family reunion when I was nine, I met my older cousins Tony and Thu who had left Vietnam before I had. They must have seen how miserable I was. The next thing I knew, I was moving to Illinois to live with my cousins. I think my aunt was relieved, and I was very happy. My life in Pasadena was not good.

My cousins were much younger and happier than my aunt. I don't know why neither was married, and I didn't ask. They let me decorate my own room and gave me privacy. I didn't have to go to church unless I wanted to.

I still miss my family even though I am happy to be in America.

Chapter 8

Faculty Meeting and Lien's Story

Tran's story stayed with me all evening. I had heard similar stories of Vietnamese mothers escaping with their children, but never one where a child was left on his own. I marveled at Tran's strength and determination to find a better life.

I had a hunch that he'd eventually share his dream with me of bringing his mother and siblings to the US as soon as he finished school. I had a further hunch that he'd do that, too!

At the extended faculty meeting that week, Tom asked each member to describe her/his idea for eliminating or reducing bigotry in the student body. Some ideas were frivolous, but a few were creative and worth considering.

After Tom recorded each idea on large sticky notes and stuck them to the white board, we voted on which should be considered seriously. The winners were:

Assign specific teams of students to research the culture of a particular immigrant population that lived in Illinois and prepare a presentation on "international day". Date TBD.

Appoint each of the bully's group to be a team leader. (I loved this one!)

On international day, ask students from other countries to bring samples of their food and explain the ingredients and how the dishes were prepared.

This last one seemed too ambitious, so I voted no, which seemed to sway the others against it.

Tom assigned himself the next step: checking the school calendar to find a good date for international day. The meeting was adjourned.

That evening in my advanced writing class, I asked my students what they would like to write about as their next assignment. Cam volunteered that the first theme deserved several more essays. "You asked us to describe an event we would never forget or someone who changed our lives. One essay is not nearly enough to cover that subject."

The other students' heads nodded in agreement. Cam continued, "Miss O'Neil, maybe we should spend this semester writing essays about these important questions. It was difficult for me to choose which important event or people I should write about. There are so many."

I asked the class: "Do you all agree?" Everyone said yes. I wondered why I hadn't anticipated their response.

I asked: "Are you familiar with the word 'memoir'?"

Thoughtful looks. Jose made a stab at the answer: "It must be something you remember."

"Right, Jose. Good start. A memoir is a book in which you write about your own life and memories. It's different from a biography which is written about someone else's life. Your essays could become a memoir, your own book of memories."

I was amazed at the response. The women clapped; the men approved with thumbs up. Writing a memoir was obviously a wonderful idea, and it wasn't even mine.

Cam asked if it had to be in chronological order. Where had she learned the word 'chronological', I wondered. "No, you can choose any order you want. For example, you can start with your arrival in the US, then go back to memories of your childhood."

*****

Lien's Story

Lien was on fire with writing her memoir, a moth to a flame. She felt driven to document her life for her two children. They were too intent on their American lives right now, but there would come a time when they would be curious about their mother's story. Who knew if she would be able to explain her past clearly when that time came. The memoir would be waiting for them. She felt grateful for Miss O'Neil's support.

Van joined me and our son Dai on leave. He arrived unexpectedly at my parents' home in a huge, chauffeur-driven jeep. I watched him jump down from the jeep and return the driver's salute then motioned him to wait. He was more handsome than before, his uniform decorated with medals and shoulder stripes. My heart danced as he walked up the path to the front door. I rushed to meet him and jumped into his arms. He laughed and held me tightly, my legs dangling.

I must have squealed because Dai ran from his room. He stopped dead and looked tentatively at me, then at his father. Van put me down, then squatted down and held out his arms to his son. Dai hesitated then flung himself at his father. Their embrace lasted a long time. I saw tears escape from Van's eyes as he held his son.

Van straightened up and used his "pretend" officer's voice: "Go pack quickly. Our car is waiting."

I was shocked. "Where are we going? What should I pack?"

"We will be staying at a friend's home on the beach. I have leave for one week."

I was thrilled. "Should I bring my little sister to watch, Dai?"

"Yes, definitely. This will give us some time to be together."

I blushed, knowing exactly how we'd spend that time. I turned to my son. "Dai, we are going on vacation with

Daddy. You may take your favorite toys and your teddy bear. Go upstairs with Auntie and she will help you pack."

Van said, "Please hurry. The driver is waiting. I don't want to waste any of our time together." I smiled and rushed upstairs. I said a quick good-bye to my family and we were on our way.

Six days later, the driver returned Dai and me to my parents' home. Van had reported back to the post. My son and I were as weepy as we had been thrilled when Van had kidnapped us. I had no idea when I would see my husband again. But I had a secret feeling that he had left something precious in my womb. A month later, I was sure of it.

I sent a letter to Van telling him that I was pregnant. He returned his message immediately. "I am so happy that we are having another child. I will arrange for you and Dai to move to Saigon. You will be near a good hospital, and it will be easier for me to visit you."

One month later, Dai and I moved into officer's quarters in Saigon. I had a chauffeur, a cook and a maid to take care of the house and Dai. My sisters were jealous, and I was thrilled. Van's two brothers and their families lived in Saigon. They invited Dai and me to their homes every week. I also knew girls from high school who had moved to Saigon, so I was not lonely. Van visited sporadically. My life was almost perfect.

Married life in the military compound was carefree. I rang a little bell when I wanted dinner served. Dai's nanny bathed him and took him on walks in our neighborhood. You would have thought that I had been raised in a wealthy family, but I hadn't. My mother had to work to help support our large family. She re-sold spices in the market.

As the wife of an officer, I was thrown into the world of officers' wives. These women were significantly older than I was. We didn't share the same interests. Their conversations about plastic surgery and love affairs bored me to tears. The endless mahjong games made me crazy.

They didn't understand why I didn't behave like a married woman. In Vietnam, once you are married, you devote yourself entirely to your family. I had the good fortune to have servants to take care of my household, leaving me free to enjoy my friends as I always had done.

Van sort of understood that I needed to follow my own life style. I told him which friends I was seeing, and he was content. We both understood that I never entered certain night clubs known as pick-up spots. As long as I shared meals with my friends, listened to music, or went to clubs where everyone joined in the singing, my husband did not object.

I was free to visit my family as often as I liked. I was happy as a married woman.

The fall of South Vietnam changed everything.

Chapter 9

Tran

My next meeting with Tran was amazing. He opened up like a rose. Sitting high up on the bleachers in the gym, we had to lean our heads together until they were nearly touching in order to hear each other over the pounding of the basketballs.

I started the conversation. "Tran, how are you getting along with the other boys?."

He answered, "Buddy's group lets me eat with them now, but they are not my friends. They are pretty stupid, but at least they're not beating me up any more."

"Do you have any real friends?" I asked.

"Not really."

I sensed he had more to say on the subject, so I remained silent. In a minute or so, Tran's words tiptoed from his mouth, "There's a girl I'd like to be friends with, but she doesn't know I exist."

"Who is she?"

Tran's voice grew a little stronger. "Hanna Lund. She's in my math and history classes. She has lots of friends and never even looks at me."

"I know Hanna. You have good taste, Tran. She's very smart and pretty. I have her in my English class."

"Wow, I didn't think you would know her."

"Well, I do. And I know her family. I taught her older sister, Megan, and her brother, Jim. Their parents are active in the PTA and always came to parents' night."

Tran looked away. I could almost hear him thinking. Finally he shifted towards me again and said in a voice I strained to hear, "Miss O'Neil, what can I do to make Hanna notice me?"

He took me by surprise. I hadn't anticipated the role of Miss Lonely Hearts and had no ready answer for him. "Let me think about it, Tran."

"Okay," he answered shyly.

I changed the subject, "Tran, do you communicate with your mother?"

"Yes, we write letters. She sends them to a friend in Paris who forwards them to me. It takes a long time."

"Does she write in English?"

"No. In Vietnamese. My cousins translate for me. I draft my letters in English and my cousins translate them into Vietnamese."

I inhaled quickly. He couldn't even communicate with his mother in the same language.

"Do you speak Vietnamese?"

"I understand most conversations. But I never learned to write it, so I don't know grammar or spelling."

"Is that Okay with you?"

"Not really. But I am an American and will live here the rest of my life, so English is more important to me. I hope to speak directly to my mother someday, and it will be in Vietnamese because she never studied English. That's why it's good for me to live with my cousins. They speak to each other in Vietnamese, so I hear it every day."

I thought this over. "What about speaking to Tony and Thu in Vietnamese, just to improve your skills?"

Tran glanced away, pondering my question. When he turned back toward me, he said enthusiastically, "That's a great idea. The three of us are so focused on being Americans, we always speak English together." I saw a mischievous smile creep around his lips. "Tonight I'm going to ask what's for dinner in Vietnamese. They will be surprised."

I left with a feeling of wonder. Here's a boy from a very different culture whose highest hope is to make a girl notice him. He's not worried about the future or how he'll pay for college or buy a car. He just wants Hanna to notice him. OMG, we are all the same deep down.

Lien's Story

Van's older brother Quan had an important job in the South Vietnamese government. When Van was home, he and his brother had private conversations in the study, with the door closed. Van never told me about these discussions, and I did not ask.

In April, 1975, South Vietnam fell to the communists. I was seven months pregnant. Van was a commander on the battlefield. I had moved Dai and myself to live with Quan's family's when Van left Saigon.

A good friend of both Van's and Quan's had hidden a 30' supply boat near the river, just in case we needed to escape. Quan returned from work one evening in early April and told me to pack an overnight bag. The rumor was that the communists were going to bomb the city the next day. I didn't panic and did exactly what I was told. It was only for one night. I packed very little – a change of clothes for me and my son and a few toiletries. I wore only a few pieces of gold jewelry.

In my heart I didn't want to go, but my brother-in-law insisted. What about Van? How would he know where we were? Part of the escape plan involved a driver who was supposed to pick up Van so he could join us on the boat.

It turned out that the roads were blocked so the driver couldn't get through to Van.

I told Dai we were going to visit a friend for the night and would be going by boat. He was excited at the prospect. I had no idea where we were really going.

None of us knew then that the president had sent his wife and children to the US several days before, along with all the gold and money they could get their hands on.

When night fell, we walked quietly to the river and joined about 95 others on the boat. The men quietly pushed the boat away from shore because the noise of the motor might have alerted the enemy to our escape. Communist soldiers were shooting anyone trying to leave the country.

I asked Quan if Van knew about the boat and their plan to leave the city. He answered no. There was no way to communicate with Van because the Red Army had cut off all communication from Saigon to the battlefield.

The boat slid noiselessly up the river. All the passengers were silent. Dai began to cry, and I rocked him until he fell asleep. One of Quan's sons raised his voice, and his mother instantly quieted him. A moment later, we heard a helicopter, then a barrage of shots. My heart began to slam in my chest. I held Dai tightly on my lap. To our amazement, we saw the helicopter fall into the river, only 50 yards from the boat.

Quan started the engine, and the boat shot toward the ocean. It was that moment that I realized we weren't leaving for one night. We were escaping from the country. I hadn't brought any food or money. I felt panic creeping through by body, but I didn't want my son and the others to see me cry.

The men on our boat were armed. When several small boats approached, our men pointed their guns at them. I knew from their faces that they would shoot if needed. All I could think was that I was leaving my husband, my parents, my family and my home. I couldn't keep the tears from spilling down my face.

We spent two terrible nights crammed together in that small boat. We had run out of gas and supplies when a barge from the US picked us up. I learned later that the barge had been picking up boat people for days. I also learned that our escape boat had been sunk by the Americans so there were no traces of our escape; and so the boat couldn't be used by the communists.

The barge was surrounded by floating bunkers, like a castle protected by a moat. On board, the boat was far from a castle. Hundreds of refugees competed for standing-room-only-space. Because I was pregnant, Dai and I were assigned space on the upper deck. We looked down at hundreds of dark heads below. I had to keep a firm grip on Dai morning, noon and night, to ensure that he didn't fall into the ocean.

The amber sun beat down on the unprotected passengers all day. The heat was stifling. At night, we were freezing. The US 7th Fleet provided some drinking *water and snacks, but not enough. A group of fishermen refugees had brought rice and cooked it on the lower deck. They gave some to Dai and the other kids and a little to me. I sold my gold bracelet to buy additional snacks. The food was gone all too soon. I felt desperate, but knew I had to be strong for my son.*

We spent three miserable days on the barge. During the day, I sat with Dai on my lap, gazing at the sea roiling with kelp. I gasped with horror when I saw water snakes as thick as a man's arm winding in and out of the kelp. Everyone knew these snakes meant instant death. I hugged Dai tightly so he wouldn't fall overboard into the snakes.

On the third day, the 7th Fleet transferred the woman and children to their ship, leaving the men behind on the barge. The sailors tied a rope to the barge to keep the two vessels close together.

One man elbowed the waiting women aside, pushing his way to the front of the line. He slipped as he lunged for the rope. I heard a crack and saw him grab his leg and let go of the rope. No one made a move as his body slid into the water. We all stared at the body and a few even smiled. I was not one of them.

My sister-in-law passed out as soon as she climbed aboard the ship. The officers immediately located Quan on the barge and air lifted both of them to an unnamed hospital. Just before my brother-in-law boarded the helicopter, he handed me his heavy bullet-proof jacket. He whispered, "All our gold is wrapped up in the pockets of this jacket. Please take care of it for me." I nodded numbly.

I was left with their three younger children, aged 13, 11 and 9, and their fortune stashed in a beat-up jacket. I rolled the jacket up and stuffed it into my overnight bag and prayed no one would steal it. It was far too hot for me to wear.

Kim, my other brother-in-law, and his family had been directed to a different ship in the 7th fleet, so we were no longer together. I was alone with four children. Nothing in my life had prepared me for this.

We were assigned to the bottom level of the ship. There were no toilets on our level. The make-shift toilets were on the top level. The only way to go from the bottom to the top was by rope ladder. I held my urine as long as I could to avoid climbing the ladder. Balancing with my protruding belly and my toddler son was terrifying. He put his little arms around my neck and held on tight, like a baby monkey, as we slowly climbed the swinging ladder. The rope cut into the soft skin of my hands.

At night, many people didn't bother with the toilets. They simply urinated in the corner, as did the children. The stench became unbearable.

On the second day when I simply had to use the toilet, I made the harrowing climb and waited patiently in the women's line. The toilets were really just shacks constructed over the ocean, with a flimsy toilet seat. There was nothing below between you and the sea.

The woman in front of me had been inside for a long time, a very long time. Finally, I went to get help. The officer shoved the door open to the toilet shack. No one was there. I guess she had fallen into the sea. The officer shrugged his shoulders and returned to his post.

From the bottom level of the ship, I could look up at the balcony one floor above. On the third day out, a man fell from the balcony and crashed into the garbage can that contained our drinking water. He died instantly. The crew disposed of his body and cleaned up the mess. I trembled the rest of that day, keeping Dai right beside me.

Everyone lined up for food three times a day. We were each given a paper plate. As we took our turn in the food line, sweaty crew members plopped scoops of unfamiliar food on our plates. It was too hot to eat much, and I didn't like the food. It was nothing I'd ever eaten before. My usual diet consisted mainly of rice and fruit and a little fish. None of these was served.

It was too hot to sleep. I spent the nights fanning myself and Dai, who had a rash all over his body. He was fretful, then grew furious. He pulled my hair and bawled. I tried to be patient and soothe him with soft words.

My nieces and nephews were mostly on their own. I simply couldn't keep track of them. The third night out, when Dai finally dozed off, I noticed that one of the nephews hadn't returned to our level to sleep. Reluctantly, I left Dai in the care of my niece and climbed the ladder.

I eventually found my nephew devouring canned tuna. He looked apologetic and explained that he was starving. Although my morning sickness was over, the smell of the canned fish was too much. I retched over the side of the ship and fumbled my way back down the ladder.

Chapter 10

Planning International Day

I wasn't surprised to find a note from Tom asking me to coordinate the International Day event. Who else, I asked myself. He advised forming a committee so I didn't end up doing everything. Good idea.

Maria, the librarian was my first choice, and she was receptive. So was Fletcher, the art teacher. My last recruit was Dana, the music teacher. He was delighted to share his love of music from various parts of the world. We met for a few minutes after school, brainstorming ideas.

I gave the committee members a short version of the Buddy/Tran incident and enjoyed their smiles when I suggested appointing each of Buddy's bully group to present facts about other countries. We decided to give the boys their choice of countries, but Buddy had to be assigned Vietnam.

Maria offered to develop a short outline of what each presenter should research. She volunteered to help the leaders complete their research every Monday at lunch and after school on Thursdays. Dana and Fletcher chimed in with time slots when the kids could confer with them about the music and art of the selected country.

"I bet I'm going to learn more than the kids," Fletcher beamed. "I'll have to get cracking so I'll look like an expert when they come to me for help." Dana nodded vigorously in agreement. Who would have thought this project would include faculty education?

Before we adjourned, Maria asked an illuminating question. "You said the bully group consisted of five boys. And that this project was to help them appreciate diversity, am I correct?"

"Yes, Tom and I thought it would be more effective than punishment, and hopefully, longer lasting."

Maria responded thoughtfully. "Then why limit it to the group of bad boys? Why not expand the number of leaders to other students who may have a genuine interest in other cultures?" Maria's soft, matronly body did not match her razor-sharp mind.

Everyone considered her proposal. I was the first to speak. "Maria, I think your idea is marvelous. We really don't know which students would appreciate an opportunity to expand their knowledge of other cultures. What do you two think?"

I knew their answers before they spoke. They were brimming with enthusiasm. Fletcher was first, "We've been looking at slides of Impressionist art in my eighth grade class. I bet someone would love to do some research on France."

Dana joined in. "I try to introduce a variety of music to the choral group. I wonder if someone would want to, say, research gospel music. Does it have to be a country? Or could it be a sub-group?"

I answered quickly. "Our goal is to broaden appreciation for people, ideas and cultures outside our traditional American experience. Why limit our students from researching anything that interests them? I'll talk to Tom."

Our little project exploded. Tom loved the idea. We chose a date two months away, with a two-hour time slot. We hoped we'd fill it with enthusiastic student presentations.

Tom announced the project over the PA the following Monday. Interested students were to drop me a note within a week with their research idea. I could hardly wait to check my cubby that afternoon. We had no idea.

Dear Miss O'Neil,

My grandparents came from Poland. I would like to make a presentation on Poland. My grandmother has offered to help me.

Marcia Kolanoski

Miss Oneel,

I want to do Japan. My great uncle was killed at Pearl Harbor.

Jimmy Poe

Miss O'Neil – I want to present Mexico. My parents were born there. My grandparents still live there.

Carmen Hernandez

Please put me down for Denmark. My favorite book when I was little was Hans Christian Anderson.

Kristen Maloney

My music teacher told us about the research project. We are singing gospel music. I love it. He said you would be Okay if I presented it.

Shavon Taylor

And on, and on. Twenty-five emails the first day; ten the following; nine the next. By Friday, 54 students had responded. I forwarded them to my committee.

Tom shared my panicked reaction when I called him at home Friday night. "What are we going to do?" he asked.

"Should we be afraid of success?" I responded tentatively, with absolutely no idea of how to deal with this.

Tom exploded, "But 54! If we limit each presentation to ten minutes, that's many, many hours. And we have to add time for one speaker to end and the other begin. Some might speak longer. I'd hate to cut someone off after they've worked hard on their presentation. Callie, we've created a monster!" I could hear the smile in his voice, along with the panic.

"Tom, let's take a deep breath and figure out how to deal with this."

"Good idea. How about meeting with your committee early Monday morning. I'll join you. Call them tonight and ask them to consider options, whatever they may be."

"OKAY, Tom. I'll do that. But I think the first step on Monday will be you on the PA saying all the time has been filled. If there are students who want to sign up, we'll do this again."

"Right. Have a nice weekend, Callie."

I slept badly Friday night. I dreamed I was jogging on the high school track and couldn't make any headway. The track was jammed with little booths displaying maps of countries from all over the world. Students stood behind each booth, all talking at once. No one was listening. And I wasn't getting any exercise.

On Monday morning, I found a note from Tran, a first. He wasn't volunteering to make a presentation.

Miss O'Neil – I think the project Mr. Picket announced is a good idea. I don't want to present about Vietnam. But I will help the student who chooses Vietnam. My cousins will, too.

Yours Truly,

Tran

I found him at lunch and thanked him for his offer, assuring him that Buddy would appreciate his help. I watched his reaction when I mentioned that Buddy's assignment was Vietnam. Without a flicker, he responded, "Yes, I can help Buddy. I am his body guard now, ha ha." All I could do was smile.

Maria was brilliant on Monday morning at the committee meeting.

"My suggestion is to designate specific days for presentations on countries within the same continent. Among the 54 volunteers, there is considerable duplication of the countries they want to research. For example, there are five students interested in France; eight for Mexico; six for England. Students interested in the same country should form a research team, each taking a distinct aspect of the culture: music, government, art, etc. I believe this will reduce the number of presentations to about 20. Still a lot, but far fewer than 54."

We all stared at her, amazed that she had reduced the problem by nearly half. Tom cleared his throat. "Thank you, Maria, for your thoughtful suggestion. I feel greatly relieved, to tell the truth." He paused. "Does anyone else have a suggestion?" No one did.

Tom continued, "Twenty presentations is still far too many for the single two-hour time slot we originally planned."

I contributed, "What if we chose two or three Saturdays? Maybe one for Europe, one for Asia and one from other continents. I bet there are lots of parents and grandparents who will be involved with this project. If we have Saturday presentations, they can come, too."

Tom grinned. "So now we have audiences of hundreds of relatives. Should we rent a convention center?" We all laughed, but knew that he was right. We'd need a large venue.

Fletcher offered, "Since it's on Saturdays, maybe my church hall would be available. The pastor is a good friend of mine. I bet he'd let us use it for free."

Tom said, "Good, Fletcher. Let Callie and me look over the calendar and get back to you with potential dates." He glanced at the clock. "It's time we got to work. I'll make the "sold out" announcement first thing."

That evening, I replied to ten more students, telling them that I'd added their ideas to the top of the list for the next time we have a cultural research project. But one message was quite different.

Dear Miss O'Neil,

I think the research project sounds very interesting. I've heard there are a lot of students who want to make presentations. If you need help organizing the kids who sign up, I will volunteer to be your assistant. My mom says I'm a good planner. I like to make lists.

Sincerely,

Hanna Lund

An instant assistant! I was delighted, and told her so in my reply. Hanna was an excellent student, precise and thorough.

And then it hit me. Tran's and Hanna's notes shared the same theme, "I'll help." And Tran wanted Hanna to notice him. Matchmaker, Matchmaker, make me a match. What if I appointed co-assistants?

Chapter 11
Cam's Story

For the first time, I thought I'd taken on far too much with my day and evening jobs. The diversity project at Acacia was consuming much too much time, at least emotionally.

My ESL job required hours of class preparation and homework review. I had added mightily to my workload with the memoir project. My advanced writing students were pouring out their memoirs faster than I could read them. I no longer had to assign papers. The students turned them in regularly, with no encouragement or deadlines from me.

Cam's latest piece intrigued me. Once I started reading the story of her brother, found myself forgetting my promise to get seven hours of sleep.

Cam's Story

Miss O'Neil:

Before you read this portion of my memoir, I've provided some background information so you will understand my brother's story.

Conflict between Catholics and Buddhists in Vietnam had been an issue since the start of French colonial rule. In a country that was 70% Buddhist, government policies were often not aligned with the needs of the people. Under Diem's Catholic regime, all Catholic lands were exempt from land reform. Catholics were given the majority of government positions, and government assistance went almost exclusively to Catholics. This persecution culminated in Hue in 1963 when a group of Buddhists, prohibited from displaying religious flags during an important holiday, sparked a riot. Eight Buddhists were killed by police. Unrest spread across the country and Diem imposed martial law in an attempt to preclude a massive riot in Saigon. Hundreds of Buddhists were arrested and murdered in the months that followed. While the conflict was partially responsible for the fall of the Diem regime, tensions between the religious groups remained.

Our father was a religious man. Our family was Buddhist. My mother was too busy raising children to focus on religion. My siblings and I worshiped at the temple every Sunday, chanting our prayers. I liked dressing up and seeing my friends more than praying. On the first and fifteenth day of the lunar calendar year, we ate only vegetables and went to the temple.

My brother, Ha, was the oldest boy in the family. He was a good son, always helping my parents with the housework and taking care of the younger children. He was not selfish like me and rarely went to parties.

When Ha graduated from high school, he got a job in a textile plant. He was a hard worker and eventually became the night shift supervisor. I remember how excited he was the first month on the job. I couldn't imagine why a job in a factory made him so happy. I asked him why he was always humming and smiling to himself. His face told me he wanted to answer but was also cautious about confiding in me.

"I promise to keep your secret," I assured him.

He pointed to the front door and motioned for me to follow him. He obviously didn't want any of our family to hear us talking. We walked down to the river and sat on my father's favorite bench.

"I've met a girl, and she is beautiful." Ha beamed. I don't think he had ever had a girlfriend before.

"Where did you meet her?"

"She works in the order office at work."

"Have you gone on a date with her?"

"Yes, several times." Ha hesitated, then whispered, "I think I'm in love."

I hugged him, which surprised and pleased him. Our family did not show affection this way. I didn't want to tell him I had been in love several times, and the *relationships usually ended once we got to know each other. I didn't want to spoil his first experience.*

"Tell me about her."

"Her name is Kim. She is modest and very pretty. We are very much alike in our devotion to our families."

"How nice," I tried to sound enthusiastic. But it didn't sound like a wildly passionate affair to me. "What else?"

Ha's glowing expression turned sorrowful. "There is a problem."

"Is she married?"

Ha's face turned from worry to horror. "Of course not! How could you think I would date a married woman?" He jumped off the seat.

"Sorry. I wasn't thinking when I asked that. What is the problem?" I knew that dating a married person wasn't all that uncommon. I'd certainly considered dating a couple of married men. But Ha would never do that.

"Sit back down and tell me what's wrong." Ha sat down, but a little further away from me.

"She's Catholic."

Neither of us spoke for a minute. My face was as grave as my brother's as we both recognized the enormity of the problem. Our father would never condone marriage to a Catholic.

"I'm sure you haven't told Dad, right?"

"Right. You know he would tell me to stop seeing her immediately. But I can't do that. I really love her."

"What are you going to do?"

"Nothing right now. It's too soon. I'm hoping that Dad will get to know her and give his permission." Both of us knew this would never happen.

"How do her parents feel about their daughter marrying a Buddhist?"

"About the same as Dad. Kim hasn't told them about me for the same reason."

We were both quiet for a few minutes, then slowly rose and walked home together. I had no solution for him.

Over the next few months, Ha continued to spend time with Kim saying he was with friends or staying late at the factory. One Saturday, he took me aside and whispered. "Kim and I are telling our parents today about our relationship and that we plan to marry."

I gulped, anticipating our father's anger. "Can I help?" I hoped he'd say no.

"That's kind of you. Would you mind being there when I tell him?"

"Okay." I wasn't happy about this, but he was my brother. I knew if the roles were reversed, he'd be there for me. "What time?"

"At 5:00, when he gets up from his nap. I'll ask him to take a walk with us."

"What about Mom?"

"She won't object. She just wants us to be happy. It's Dad I'm worried about."

As you should be, I thought. But I said, "Okay, I'll be home at 5:00." I decided to prepare for the confrontation by meeting my girl friends for tea, then some shopping. But all afternoon I was distracted.

As if it had been scripted, Dad exploded when Ha told him about his plans to marry a Catholic. Dad ignored Ha's pleas to at least meet her and see for himself what a wonderful young woman she was. "How can you possibly marry a Catholic when you know how they have mistreated the Buddhists? How corrupt they've made the government? How they discriminate against all Buddhists?" he roared.

Ha tried to placate him. "Dad, what you say about the Catholics is true. But I'm not marrying a government official. Kim is a kind, loving woman. She's not responsible for people in powerful positions. She's just an order department clerk."

Our father wouldn't listen and stomped home alone, turning his back on us.

"Well, that turned out just as we expected," I commented. Then I saw Ha's tears. My heart went out to him. "Ha, your happiness is more important than Dad's anger. Don't let him ruin your life."

He opened his eyes, brushed the backs of his hands across his cheeks, and said, "You are right, Cam. Kim and I will marry with or without our parents' permission. I would prefer to have their blessing, but if that is not possible, we will marry anyway." I assured him I would come to their wedding.

And that's exactly what happened. Ha and Kim were married without either set of parents in attendance. Kim's sister and brother came. And of course, I came. Several friends joined us at a modest reception. The bride and groom were glowing. We all knew without saying it aloud that they were smiling though the pain of not having their parents share the happiest day of their lives.

Chapter 12
Buddy and Tran

Buddy had always been big for his age, which made adults and some kids think he was older than he was and expect him to behave the way an older boy would. He continually failed to meet their expectations. He was an immature boy in an older boy's body.

It seemed the only way to take advantage of his size was to bully smaller boys. His "gang" automatically acknowledged him as the leader, although he was poorly equipped to lead himself and pitifully unqualified to lead others.

True to his word, at lunch the week after the project had been closed to more students, Tran offered to help Buddy with his Vietnam research project. Buddy shuffled his feet and looked away when he muttered, "Thanks." Mr. Picket had told Buddy personally that he had been assigned Vietnam as his country. Buddy knew enough not to argue.

Tran rode his bike to Buddy's house the following Saturday to work on the project. He approached the huge two-story house cautiously and rang the doorbell. Buddy answered immediately and ushered Tran into the kitchen where he introduced Tran to his parents who politely greeted the small boy. Tran saw the raised eyebrows look Buddy's mother exchanged with his father, who merely shrugged his shoulders and turned back to his newspaper. The boys went upstairs to Buddy's room.

Tran thought he'd entered Dick's Sporting Goods. Baseball bats, gloves and balls were on one shelf. Two tennis rackets were propped against the wall. A hockey stick against another. A pile of athletic shoes took up an entire corner of the room. A large wire basket held a basketball, two soccer balls, tennis ball cans, and a volley ball.

Tran said in amazement, "Where did you get all this equipment? I didn't know you played all these sports."

Buddy looked miserable. "I don't. It's my dad. He played varsity volleyball and ran cross country in school. He's still on an adult soccer team. Every birthday and Christmas he gives me sports equipment."

"Can you play any of these sports?" Tran asked.

Buddy hung his head and muttered, "Not really. I'm not good at anything."

Tran didn't know what to say, so he was silent. He looked around the room and saw a desk covered with papers, empty soda cans, and a partially completed model airplane.

"Is this where you do homework?" Tran pointed to the desk.

"Un huh. I do it in the kitchen. My mom helps me."

"Where can we work on the project?" Tran realized that they'd need a clean space.

"I dunno. Let's ask my mom." Buddy led the way out of the sports store, yelling, "Mom, where can we do the project?"

Buddy's mom appeared at the bottom of the stairs. "What's wrong with your room?"

"It's full of stuff."

"Why don't you clean it up then?" Tran thought her question was reasonable, but saw Buddy's face redden and his fist clench.

"I don't have time! Tran's here now. Where can we sit?" Buddy demanded.

His mother looked exasperated. Tran couldn't keep himself from comparing Buddy's belligerent behavior and ugly tone of voice with the quiet, respectful way he and his cousins spoke to each other.

"Use the dining room, as long as you clean up after yourself," she sounded reluctant but resigned. Without thanking her, Buddy stomped past his mother motioning Tran to follow. Tran tried a tiny smile as he stepped carefully in front of Buddy's mother. He said quietly, "Thank you." Buddy's mother looked surprised, then smiled in return. "You're welcome." She turned and disappeared down the hallway.

The dining room contained a huge table with elaborate silver candlesticks lined in a row down the center of the table. Before Tran could stop him, Buddy knocked them down, and they crashed to the hardwood floor. Buddy's mother came flying into the room. "What was that?" she yelled.

"Those stupid candles. We need room to spread out."

His mother was speechless. Tran began to collect the silver pieces and uprooted candles, but Buddy grabbed Tran's shoulder. "She can do that when we're through."

Tran had seen enough. He looked directly at Buddy and spoke firmly. "Buddy, if we're going to work together, we need to agree on some rules. The first is to treat your mother with respect. The next is to clean up your mess and not destroy your home. Please help me collect these things."

Both mother and son were stunned. Buddy raised his right fist and glared at Tran. His mother stepped back, anticipating Buddy's typical reaction when he was confronted. Tran didn't flinch.

Tran's voice was low and even, "Either you agree or I leave. Make your choice, Buddy. I'm not kidding." Buddy slowly dropped his arm, and Tran heard Buddy's mother exhale.

"Okay," Buddy said reluctantly and began to collect the fallen objects. Buddy's mother watched the boys collect the candlesticks. They didn't see the gleam in her eyes.

Tran placed a copy of the librarian's outline in front of Buddy. "Where do you want to start? Tran asked.

"I dunno. I don't know anything about Vietnam."

Tran noticed that Buddy lost his bravado when there wasn't a crowd around to impress. In fact, he appeared nervous and unsure of himself. Tran thought he should be happy to see Buddy so lost for a change, but he wasn't.

Chapter 13

Cam and Ha

Cam was obsessed with her memoir. She needed to leave a record of her life for her children when they were older.

As soon as the kids were doing homework or bathing or sleeping, Cam rushed to her desk and wrote. She winced when she considered the quick meals she'd been serving for weeks now, just to conserve time and get back to her desk. Well, Americans have been eating mac and cheese for decades, and they seemed to flourish, she rationalized. Thank you, Trader Joe's.

Cam wondered if she could have a draft completed before her family reunion that summer. That gave her three months. She could leave blanks for details of the older family members and fill them in at the reunion. Her grandfather, aunts and uncles seemed uncomfortable on the phone. The only time she tried to interview them remotely on the phone, they said that someone could be listening in, recording the conversation. Cam didn't argue. She thought she'd be more successful face-to-face anyway.

She hoped Miss O'Neil wouldn't think she was trying to drown her with chapters that hadn't been assigned, but she couldn't help herself. Her story had been waiting for years to spill out of her heart.

She'd made an outline, as Miss O'Neil had suggested. It included each major phase and event of her life. She intended to finish her brother Ha's story this week. She loved putting a check mark on the outline as she completed each chapter.

My brother Ha and his wife Kim celebrated their 22nd anniversary last year. Their three children went with them to New York for a long weekend of sightseeing, a show at Radio City Music Hall, oysters at Grand Central Station, and long walks through Central Park.

Their oldest daughter, Julie, seemed distracted but happy on the anniversary trip. She was a paralegal at a large law firm in Chicago.

Ha and Kim knew Julie had been dating the same white American since her junior year at the University of Chicago. Jim was an upstanding person and was now doing well financially as a stock broker. The problem with Jim was that he wasn't Catholic. Ha and Kim were devoted to the Church. Ha had converted two years after marrying Kim, and their entire social life revolved around St. Paul's.

Julie had brought Jim home for several holidays, and her family seemed to like him. When Jim had invited

Julie to meet her parents, Ha refused his permission to let her accept. Julie knew why. In Vietnam, when a girl visits her boyfriend's home, it means her family agrees to an engagement.

She didn't know how to tell her parents they wanted to be engaged. She called me to ask how to handle this difficult situation. I suggested she wait until the end of the New York trip, then respectfully ask her father's permission to accept Jim's proposal.

Julie followed my advice. While they waited at the airport for their planes, Julie told her parents she had something important to discuss. She saw her parents exchange a guarded look. Her mother looked at her lap, and her father asked what was this important thing. Julie hesitated, took in a deep breath, and in a low respectful voice told them she wanted to accept Jim's marriage proposal.

Her father immediately responded, "I can't give you permission to marry a non-Catholic. This is final." He stood up. Julie looked beseechingly at her mother who continued to study the floor. Julie burst into tears and rushed to the restroom. She didn't come out until she heard her parents' flight called.

Julie's voice wavered when she called me from Chicago. "What should I do?" I could hear the misery in her voice.

"Ask once again, but this time be more firm. Tell him that you want his blessing, but you intend to marry Jim with or without it."

"Can I do that?" Julie's voice was timid, childlike.

"That's what you're intending, right?"

"Yes, but I've always been so close to my parents. I'm grateful for all they've sacrificed for me, for my sister and my brother. I've never gone against their wishes."

I knew she was suffering. "Julie, I need to remind you that your father married your mother without either of their parents attending the ceremony. It was a bitter sweet day for both of them. I'm amazed that my brother doesn't sympathize with you since he was in exactly the same position."

"I've thought the same thing, but it would be rude of me to mention this. It would show such disrespect."

I knew typical American kids wouldn't hesitate to throw the past in their parents' faces. Julie's reaction reflected the charm and the frustration of mixed cultures.

Reluctantly, I said, "Okay, I'll call your father tomorrow evening and remind him gently about his past. And I'll assure him you will marry Jim with or without his blessing. It would break your mother's heart not to attend her first daughter's wedding."

Julie gushed, "Thank you, thank you, Auntie Cam. I would be so grateful. Please call me as soon as you've talked to him." I assured her I would.

The next day after work I called Ha. "Brother, I talked to Julie yesterday. She was crying because you have refused your permission to marry Jim."

Ha's voice was stern. "That is correct. I do not want her to marry a non-Catholic."

"I understand. But this is Julie's life, and she loves Jim. Do you think he is a good man?"

"Yes, but he is Protestant."

"Ha, you were Buddhist. Do you remember how your father and Kim's father refused their permission for your marriage?"

Silence. I let a minute pass, then asked gently, "Do you remember?"

Ha's voice softened. "Yes, I remember. But that was before I converted to Catholicism."

"Do you want Julie to be married without her parents being there?"

He didn't answer. I continued without raising my voice. "Ha, Julie and Jim are going to marry. They want to have a family. I know how much you love children. How will you explain to your grandchildren why you were not at their mother's wedding?"

I heard Ha sigh. "Sister, I will think about this. And I will pray for guidance."

I smiled. The grandkids had been the trump card. I have just learned about trump cards. They are very important.

Chapter 14

International Day

I went to the library at lunch, hoping to catch Maria for an update on how the kids were doing with their diversity research. She wasn't at the front desk, but I spotted one pepper and one salt head bowed close together at a work table. Their backs were to me, but I recognized Tran and Hanna.

My co-assistants appeared to be working diligently on an oversized sheet of drawing paper. I couldn't see the details. I smiled to myself that Tran had been granted his wish. Hanna had noticed him. I turned quickly and left the room.

Fletcher, Maria, Dana and I were flooded with student requests to help them with their presentations. Dana, in particular, was working overtime, ordering music from all over the world. His face looked sallow, I guessed from lack of sleep, but he wasn't complaining. In fact, I'd never seen him look happier.

You could never tell about Maria. She kept her emotions under wraps. But it was difficult to find her without at least a couple of kids asking for advice. I decided to wait until our committee met to get a progress report.

Fletcher's desk was piled with oversized books featuring artists from Asia, Europe and Africa. I heard him humming as he marked pages with colored tabs.

So far, there were no crises. Fletcher's pastor had come through with the church hall. The Asian countries presentations were scheduled two weeks from Saturday. We had no idea how many students and family members would attend, so the pastor offered to leave the standard set up of 100 chairs.

We asked for a table to be set up for the presenter at the far end of the hall. There was a small work room behind this area where I could lurk in case a presenter needed help at the last minute. Thankfully, there was a partial wall separating the work area from the main hall, so I wouldn't be spotted.

Tran and Hanna attended the final committee meeting. They were both terribly serious as they handed out copies of the sheet I'd seen them working on. Tran cleared his throat and began to speak without being prompted.

"Hanna and I have drafted a schedule of the presentations on Asian countries. There will be seven presentations. This schedule lists the countries and the presenters. Hanna will now discuss the order."

Hanna hopped off her chair and faced the committee members. "Tran and I agreed that Buddy should go first, since this whole idea started with him."

Tran interrupted, "And besides, Buddy is so nervous that he has to go first. If he has to wait, he'll get stage fright and might leave the building."

The committee members nodded assent, trying to keep their expressions neutral, which was difficult. I knew we were all howling with laughter inside, picturing Buddy's noisy, clumsy stampede from the church hall.

"That's very wise," I assured the assistants with a straight face. Hanna continued with a detailed list of presenters.

"I'll be hiding in the little room just behind the presenters," I told everyone. Hanna nodded and said that some of the kids were planning mixed media presentations that could require assistance. Oh my, now I was the A/V tech. Perhaps I'd ask Tom to join me in the work room since he was a slide projector expert.

*****

Two weeks flew by. Presenters missed some homework assignments and looked exhausted but excited. I wondered if we were doing the right thing. But there was electricity in every classroom. Most teachers were incorporating information about the Asian countries since those presentations were scheduled for the following Saturday.

There weren't enough chairs! Saturday at 9:00 the hall started filling up, way before the 10:00 start time.

The pastor was standing by, and at 9:30 he and some of the parents added a few more rows of chairs. By 9:55, there was standing room only. Tom and I were amazed and delighted to see grandparents, siblings, babies and many of our students enter the hall.

Buddy had certainly cleaned up his appearance, but his face was chalk. He and Tran were huddled behind the presenters' table, apparently going over last minute details. Tran wore a dress shirt that was too big, and a string tie from another era. He appeared calm. I noticed him placing a chair behind the presenters' table. Apparently, he intended to be right near in case Buddy needed him.

At exactly 10:00 Tom greeted the audience and explained that this was the first of three Saturdays where students would present information about other countries and cultures. He did not include the genesis of the project, but focused on the importance of recognizing the contributions of immigrants in the US throughout our history.

Hanna spoke next. She was poised and lovely in a flowered dress and low white heels. She named each speaker and country in the order of presentation, then handed the mic to Tran.

Tran's voice was so low the audience had to lean forward to hear him as he introduced Buddy. "Buddy is the first presenter. He will speak about Vietnam. My family is from Vietnam, but this is not why Buddy is first. It's because this will be the first time Buddy has done something like this, and he wants to get it over with." The parents burst out laughing and a few clapped.

Tran turned back to the table and sat erectly in the chair facing the audience. Buddy spoke into the mic. "I want to thank Tran for helping me with this project. And also his cousins Tony and Thu." Light applause. I couldn't see Tony or Thu from my hiding place behind the partition, but I knew they were there.

Buddy began, "Vietnam is a long narrow country in South East Asia. It is run by communists."

His voice was drowned out by the pounding of someone heavy running toward the speakers' table. Tom and I shot out from our hiding place to see Mr. Jones, the surly father at our meeting weeks ago, hurling himself toward Buddy, a gun in his hand. "Vietnam's a god-damned communist hell hole!" he screamed. "And you ain't gonna pretend it's anything but that."

He jerked Tran from his chair, grabbed the boy in a choke hold and shoved the gun against his head, facing the crowd. The audience gasped then went silent, stunned. Buddy started toward the maniac, but Mr. Jones shouted, "One step closer and I'll shoot this gook, just like I killed his relatives in Vietnam." Buddy froze.

Tom and I were behind the mad man. I took tiny, slow steps back behind the partition, then flew out the back door frantically dialing 911 on my cell. "There's an armed maniac at the Baptist church." My voice was strangled.

"We know where you are. Now calm down. What is happening? Take a deep breath."

I did, then tried to speak slowly. "An armed man has taken a boy hostage in the church hall and has a gun pointed to his head. There are dozens of people here. We're afraid he'll shoot the boy if we take action."

"Help is already on the way." The officer's voice was calm. "Keep him talking. Can you do that?"

"I guess so," I stammered, then added, "Tell the rescue team to enter the back of the hall. The mad man's back is to that door."

"Roger that. Now go back and start talking."

I was shaking so hard I slammed my knee against the hall door as I re-entered the building. Mr. Jones swung around to face me. "I remember you, bitch! You're the one who made my son apologize for attacking the gook here."

I looked straight at him, but kept my distance so he wouldn't think I was trying to rescue Tran.

"I'm Miss O'Neil. Yes, I was the one who found Tran bleeding on the floor." My voice was shaking, but I held my head up.

"He's lucky he wasn't killed like he deserves." He tightened his hold on Tran's neck. Tran's face was expressionless and pale. His body was absolutely still. Buddy was sobbing, but too panicked to move. I heard soft footsteps coming toward us from the audience, but didn't break eye contact with the mad man to see who was approaching.

"Were you in Vietnam?" I asked. Keep him talking, I told myself.

"Yes, you idiot. I left my right leg there to prove it. And I left dead buddies there, too. They died for nothing."

"How long were you there?"

He screamed at me, "What difference does that make, bitch! Long enough to hate the bastards hiding in the jungle, attacking us at night, sending kids in with explosives. And when we came home, were you and your kind there to give us a parade? To thank us for risking our lives? Where the hell were you? You and Jane Fonda." He finally glanced at the audience, including them in his tirade.

At exactly the moment Mr. Jones looked at the audience, the back door crashed open and the rescue team poured in. Jones was grabbed from behind and pinned to the ground by two armed men. Tony had been creeping toward us and ran to Tran as Mr. Jones' gun dropped from his hand. He scooped the boy up and cradled him against his chest as if he were a baby. I saw Tran's shoulders heaving as he sobbed against his cousin's shirt as Tony carried him out of the room.

The parents and students stood in stunned silence as Mr. Jones was dragged out the back door. Tom slowly retrieved the mic and addressed them. "Please join me in a prayer to thank God or whoever you worship for saving Tran's life."

The moment of silence seemed endless. I couldn't keep my sobs inside any longer. I turned my back on the scene and began to cry. I felt a gentle hand on my arm and turned to find Thu, face pale and streaked with tears. "Please come to our home with me." I stumbled to where Tony and Tran waited for us in the car.

Chapter 15

Recovery

I collapsed on the coach, sobbing while Tran and Thu patted me. They were amazingly calm and kind. They arranged pillows on the sofa and covered me with a quilt. I cried for hours. I heard soft footsteps all though the night.

I don't know what time I finally drifted off to sleep. I awoke to a laser of sunlight across the quilt and soft voices murmuring in the kitchen. I found the bathroom, tried unsuccessfully to tame my hair, and used the new tooth brush thoughtfully placed on the sink. My face was a wreck, but I didn't care. Tran was safe. No one was hurt. At least not physically.

"Thank you for your kindness last night," I said in a shaky voice to Tony and Thu when I joined them in the kitchen. Neither looked rested. Tony inclined his head in response. Thu patted my shoulder. How amazing that they were the ones comforting me when their nephew had been the victim!

"Where is Tran?" I asked.

"He's still sleeping," Thu answered. "He was awake several times last night."

Tony added, "We are going to call his mother later today. He'll feel better when he hears her voice." I wondered how Tran would communicate his experience to his mother who didn't speak English.

"I should go home now. I'm sure the police will want a report."

Tony offered to drive me home, and I accepted gratefully. "How do you feel, Tony?" I asked once we were on our way.

"Grateful that Tran is Okay."

"Will this change the way you and Thu take care of Tran?"

"No. What can we change? There are crazy people in every country. Especially people who have gone to war."

I considered his answer. "Will you be afraid for Tran in the future?"

Tony glanced at me, then back at the road. "Tran is a strong boy. He will be fine."

I didn't know what to say, so I was silent. When we pulled up to my building, Tony spoke again. "If you have time, I would appreciate your help with writing."

"I'm not sure what you mean," I answered, startled by the change of subject.

"I need to learn to write business letters. My English classes were for speaking. Do you have time?"

"I will make time, Tony. I'll call you soon and set up a time." I was amazed he could think about writing correspondence after what had just happened. He was stronger than I was by a long shot.

There were nine messages on my machine, two from the police, three from Tom, one from Buddy's mother, one from Maria, one from Dana, and one from Fletcher.

After a hot bath, I began to respond to the messages, starting with the police. Maria's and Dana's messages offered condolences. But Fletcher's was different. He said something about his experience teaching Vietnamese refugees in San Francisco right after the war, and that he'd tell me about it after thing calmed down. I was too tired to think about it.

*****

Tom scaled back on the diversity project. He reserved one hour a week for presentations in the cafeteria. No outsiders. There wasn't enough time to complete them this year, but no one seemed to care. Both students and faculty were subdued, knowing they had literally dodged a bullet.

The police department sent a psychologist to speak to the student body. She offered to meet with individuals on request. Tom showed me a list of families that had signed up for individual sessions with her. Buddy's name was first. Tran's was not included.

I called Tony at home to ask if he and Thu wanted to meet with the psychologist; and to ask if Tran would be interested.

Tony responded. "We are fine. Please remember that we survived a war. Thu and I have seen far more terrible things than Mr. Jones."

I tried to process this information, but knew I would probably never understand what they had experienced, at least, I hoped I wouldn't.

"How is Tran?"

Tony's voice was softer. "He is studying hard."

That wasn't what I was asking, and I think Tony knew it. I tried again. "Is Tran sleeping well? Does he eat normally?"

"Don't worry about Tran. He is a strong boy."

"Did Tran talk to his mother?"

"Yes."

I had to drag out answers to my questions. "Do you think the conversation made him feel better?"

Tony was thoughtful. "His mother doesn't speak English, so I had to translate. I told her what happened and she was upset. She asked me to ask Tran if he was Okay."

"What did Tran say?" already guessing the answer.

"He said he was fine. That the man had not shot him."

I was shocked. That was all, he hadn't been shot. I immediately began to imagine what Tran might have wanted to say if they spoke the same language,

Mom, I was terrified. A crazy man shoved a gun to my head. He was choking me, so I was afraid to move. I just stayed calm and quiet so he wouldn't shoot me. I've never been so scared in my life. I wish I could see you. I wish I were home.

Tony paused, I guess giving me time to think. He finally asked me softly, "Have you found time to teach me English writing?"

I exhaled. "Well, I could find time on the weekends. Would that work for you?"

"Certainly, I will be available whenever you have time."

"How about Sunday afternoon at 2:00?" I didn't know if they went to church in the morning. And Saturday was my day for errands, house cleaning, and all the things I skipped during the week.

"Sunday will be fine. Where should we meet?"

I thought quickly. "We can meet either at your house or my apartment. Which would you prefer?"

Tony didn't answer immediately. I waited. "At your apartment. I will be able to focus all my attention if I am not at home."

"Fine, Tony. Please bring examples of the types of documents you need to respond to."

"I will. Thank you."

"You're welcome. See you Sunday."

*****

Fletcher and I finally ended up in the faculty room at the same time. The minute he saw me, he said, "Callie, I have something to show you. I'll just be a minute. It's in my desk." And he bolted out the door.

He returned carrying an old-fashioned-looking scrapbook with yellow pages hanging outside the dusty cover. "What is this, Fletcher?"

"Did you know that I taught grammar school in the Tenderloin in San Francisco after the war?"

"No, I didn't."

"I was the roving art teacher and worked with every grade in a battered old school in one of the worst neighborhoods in the City. There were children from Vietnam, Laos and Cambodia who were just off the boat, so to speak."

I wondered where this story was going, but he'd already piqued my interest.

"I've heard you talking to Maria about your ESL class' project of writing their memoirs, so I thought you'd find this art work relevant." He opened the cover lovingly, careful not to tear the fragile pages.

"What is that?" I asked in alarm. The pencil drawing was of a tree, just the way a five-or-six-year-old would draw it. A trunk and spidery branches, no leaves or the other details older children would have added. But in the center of the tree was a person, standing straight up, its feet not resting on a branch. Just upright in the air, but in the tree.

"It's a ghost," Fletcher said sadly. It did not look like an American ghost. There was no round head and trailing pillow case body. It looked like a person. A live person.

Fletcher turned the page. There were more ghost/people in trees drawn by different children. Fletcher had carefully printed each artist's name under his or her picture. Fletcher's eyes were full of pain. "These ghosts were people fleeing the North Vietnamese army. They climbed trees and died of starvation. The children saw them every day."

He turned another page. This one had a title, "***Mommy***."

Fletcher's voice began to quiver. "I thought your Vietnamese students might include these ghosts in their memoirs, and I wanted you to understand why the children remembered."

I didn't know what to say, so I murmured, "Thank you, Fletcher. I'm grateful to you for showing me these tragic pictures."

117

His sadness lifted as he handed me a smaller lined notebook. "This book is from the same school, but from fourth and fifth graders. They were also from Southeast Asia and had escaped with their families." The first page was framed by faded red, white and blue flags drawn as a border. The printing under the flags said: "I love America. I am free." The following pages offered similar positive messages.

"You see, Callie, these are resilient people. Your advanced writing students may have drawn pictures like these when they first came to the US. Now they're writing their memoirs. I wish I were that strong. I wish I were as strong as young Tran." His eyes welled – I guessed for the evil that children had been exposed to and the violence Tran had just endured.

Fletcher and I never talked about this again, but our relationship changed that day. I knew we had made a bond and would be there for each other.

Chapter 16

Sundays

At exactly 2:00 on Sunday, the building door buzzer went off. I did what I always did and asked, "Who is it?"

Tony's voice was subdued. "It's Tony for my lesson." I pushed the release button and told him how to find my apartment.

He knocked softly on my door, even though I had left it open. He shuffled his feet self-consciously, seemingly reluctant to come in. He held out a bunch of daisies without saying a word.

"How thoughtful of you, Tony. Please come in. We can sit at the table. Let me find a vase for the flowers. I love daisies." His smile did not reach his black eyes which remained tense and wary. When he sat down, his back was straighter than the chair, his polished shoes carefully placed together under the table.

I tried to identify why he was so uncomfortable, particularly in light of the trauma we had experienced together. And then it hit me. He was a single man visiting a single woman. I wondered if in his culture, this had far more significance than it did to native-born Americans.

Food. According to my mother, you could always get what you wanted if you fed a man. It hadn't worked for my marriage, but I couldn't think of an alternative. I headed for my small kitchen. "Tony, would you mind if we had something to eat before we started? I haven't had time for lunch."

He looked surprised, but answered courteously. "Of course, you should eat if you're hungry."

"Would you mind coming in the kitchen for a minute?" He dutifully stood and followed me. "Have you eaten?" I asked.

"I had breakfast this morning. But I'm a little hungry."

I opened the refrigerator and motioned for him to take a look. "Let's find something interesting. What looks good to you?" He glanced at the shelves. Fortunately, I had shopped the day before, and there were actual choices, which was often not the case.

Tony offered, "I can make us stir fry. Would you like that?"

I told him that would be perfect. He smiled warmly for the first time and went to work. I just sat on a stool and watched him. Who knew I'd have a personal chef? And one who insisted on cleaning up after we ate his delicious dish.

"Tony, that was wonderful. Who taught you to cook?"

"My mother. She didn't really teach me. I watched her cook for our family.

When Thu and I got older, we cooked for our four younger siblings when my mother went to market."

"Do you mean when she went shopping?"

"No, she baked and sold cakes at the market in our village. She was gone for many hours."

Another story to capture, I thought. But all in good time.

When we sat beside each other for the lesson, Tony seemed relaxed and happy. Maybe my mother knew more than I gave her credit for. But I knew she'd be surprised to see the man doing the cooking. It worked for me!

*****

I found myself looking forward to Sundays. Tony was an excellent student. His writing was a little stilted, but he communicated his message clearly and grammatically. As rewarding as his progress was to me as his teacher, I admitted to the mirror that I also enjoyed his company. I went shopping for new Sunday afternoon outfits.

On the fourth Sunday afternoon, Tony surprised me by gently kissing me when I opened the door. I surprised myself by enthusiastically returning his kiss. I kicked the door shut, and we clung to each other. It was a while before we began our lesson. All afternoon we found ourselves glancing at each other in wonder. We ended the afternoon with glasses of Chardonnay from one of my favorite Sonoma wineries. Sunday became my favorite day of the week.

After two more sessions, I think we both realized there was no more need for private writing lessons. Yet neither of us said a word about stopping. Our greetings, wine tasting and good-byes were taking up as much time as the writing lessons.

I found myself daydreaming about Tony during the week. Did he like to travel? Did he sleep on his back or his side? What was his favorite movie? And on and on. I realized how little I knew about his past. I knew far more about Cam and Lien.

The next Sunday I asked him about immigrating and growing up in the US.

His uncle had worked in the Office of the Secretary of State for the South Vietnamese government. Their family was one of the lucky ones airlifted in the early days of the war. His uncle offered to sponsor Tony's family, but it was too late. His father had served in the South Vietnamese army and died in combat. His mother didn't have the heart or language skills to leave, but she encouraged Tony and Thu to immigrate. She assured them the younger siblings would take care of her.

So Tony and Thu immigrated to the US and lived with their uncle's family. Tony had paper routes. Thu baby-sat Vietnamese neighbors' kids on weekends. They learned English, but Thu struggled with conversation. Her reading and writing came far more easily than speaking.

When he paused in his story, I asked him if he'd like a drink. By then I knew his favorite was iced coffee with a splash of milk and one lump of sugar. He accepted gratefully.

"I went to junior college, then transferred to State, where I earned a business degree. I got a break in finding work. I have a cousin who imports and exports shoes. One of his suppliers offered me a job, and I jumped at it. I've been working there ever since."

"Have you considered other professions?" I asked.

Tony looked gravely at me. "Yes, I have. Let's talk about this another time."

"Okay," I agreed. I sensed he would tell me more when he was ready.

*****

On the first Sunday in June, the last week of school, Tony asked about my plans for the summer. I told him I would continue teaching adult classes, and that I'd been thinking about doing some traveling but had no firm plans.

I recognized his thoughtful look by then. A slight knitting of his eyebrows, downward glance, then direct eye contact when he was ready. "I would like to extend an invitation." I had never heard him use "extend" before, so I suspected he had rehearsed this speech.

"Okay, what is it, Tony?"

"Cam's family is having a reunion in California next month. Since she is our cousin, Thu, Tran and I will attend. We would like you to go with us."

I was stunned. How would a non-family member, a white woman, fit in at a Vietnamese family reunion? Tony read my puzzled reaction and removed an envelope from his notebook. I recognized Cam's lovely handwriting.

Dear Miss O'Neil,

Tony was supposed to give you this note after asking you to attend our family reunion. You have given our family so much joy. We want to reciprocate. (I hope this is the right word.) Please come! Our family will welcome you. They are very excited to meet you.

Your friend,

Cam

I couldn't help smiling at the warmth and sincerity emanating from both Cam and Tony. "Thank you so much, Tony. Being including in your family celebration is very special to me." I surprised myself when I felt my eyes filling. Tony gently used his thumbs to wipe my tears away.

I cleared my throat and took a small step back. "I promise to think about it."

After Tony left, I had one of my talks with myself. There were distinct disadvantages of living alone at times like this. No one to talk to; no one to tell you that you're crazy; or that you should trust your instincts.

I looked in the mirror and spoke out loud. "Callie, you are very attracted to a Vietnamese immigrant, aren't you?" I nodded slowly to my image. "I thought so. What the hell do you think you're doing?"

I shrugged, the universal gesture that said I haven't a clue. I turned abruptly from the mirror and answered myself. I don't have to know where I'm going. I'm just living one day at a time. And I'm going to the reunion.

I resisted returning to the mirror to make the terrible face my sister had taught me – thumbs pulling my mouth wide, index fingers on my nose, and crossing my eyes.

Chapter 17
Cam's Story

I never thought I would return to Vietnam and see my family again. We exchanged letters, clumsily. I would write my parents and send the letter to an escapee friend in France. She would re-route the letter in a new envelope and send it to Vietnam. It took up to two months to arrive.

My family lost everything under the communists. Because my family had been involved in the South Vietnamese government, they were considered the bottom of the pot. After the communists took control, my mother still earned a little money cooking and selling food. It was important that my family had always been considered "good," or they would have suffered even more.

I had followed my father's advice and become a teacher. Under the communists, I had no choice of jobs and, as punishment, was sent to a town near the ocean, a seven-hour drive from my family. I dated a fellow teacher named Binh, who was from a wealthy family. We wanted to escape to the USA, like so many others had done.

We didn't tell our parents about our plans. Our first step was a hasty marriage in our hometown. Then we went to the beach, pretending to simply be enjoying the sun and the water. A boat was hidden nearby, but we had to wait until dark to sneak aboard. We hid in the bushes for hours, waiting for darkness, but two soldiers patrolled the beach. We didn't make it to the boat. We returned to our teaching jobs in the country.

The Communists were always watching us. They knew we wanted to escape. We formulated a bold new plan. When the school term ended, we returned to our home near the coast. My husband walked to the river one day in plain sight. The men on patrol knew he wouldn't escape without me, but he did! He took my father's small rowboat out as if he were going fishing. He never returned. A larger boat was waiting for him where the river meets the ocean.

Two months later I escaped while on vacation in Thailand. I ended up in Macau. Binh was in the Philippines. He had family members who had found sponsors and immigrated to Australia. He wanted me to meet him there, since the sponsors agreed to include both of us, the newly married couple. I refused to go. I had dreamed of living in the US.

My cousins Tony and Thu tried to sponsor me, but that didn't work because I was married. My plan was to get to the US, then sponsor Binh. But the waiting list to enter the US was very long. Australia would accept both of us immediately. I waited two years in Macau, and then finally joined Binh in Australia. It wasn't a total waste of time because I studied English.

We lived in Sydney for several years. My husband went to night school to learn English. He worked in a factory during the day. I studied English during the day. Binh became a welder, but he missed teaching school. We couldn't afford to have him start university all over again, and his accent was very strong. He was afraid that children wouldn't understand him in the classroom.

I worked as a part-time waitress in a cocktail bar, sometimes very late at night. I got good tips.

Binh's company was international with a plant in Canada. His boss offered him a transfer to that plant. We were so happy to move because we had not forgotten our dream of living in the US. Canada was much closer than Australia.

As soon as we settled in Canada, we added our names to the US immigration list. We waited five years before we were accepted. In the meantime, we had two children. Our Vietnamese friends watched my children for two hours while I was in class. I watched their children at night when they went to school. The immigrant community became our family.

Our children were native English speakers. We did not speak Vietnamese at home because we wanted them to consider English as their first language. I continued to study English and felt confident in speaking and reading.

We were able to sponsor my sister and her family when they left Vietnam. They still live in Canada. They were sad when we moved to America, but we see each other at new years.

*****

The timing of the family reunion was perfect for Cam's latest addition to her memoir. I had no idea she had lived in Australia and Canada. So many of my adult students had harrowing stories! I wondered if I would ever have had the patience to spend years in "temporary" countries.

As I read her story, I started to become excited about the upcoming reunion. I was anxious to hear other stories from Cam's family members. The event would take place in Pasadena, California, near Los Angeles. I had called a college friend whose husband taught at Cal Tech, and she responded immediately with a promise to show me around. She invited me to stay in their guest cottage. I told her I wasn't sure about housing just yet, but thanked her for the generous offer.

Maybe I'd need a place to get away from the family. Or maybe they'd like some time by themselves, so staying "off site" might be perfect. I'd have to talk to Cam and Tony, or just play it by ear.

Cam came a little late to class the following week, so we didn't have a chance to talk. I asked if she could stay for a few minutes after class, and she readily agreed.

When the others had left, I returned her latest piece with some suggestions. Then I accepted her invitation and told her how honored I felt to be invited to her family reunion. I was touched to see the happiness sparkling in her eyes. She hugged me quickly and couldn't speak for a minute. She covered her mouth with her hand and looked away. I busied myself with some paperwork.

Once she had composed herself, she thanked me for agreeing to come and said that it meant a great deal to her and to her family to have me join them.

"Would you like to drive with us to Los Angeles?" she asked.

"No, thank you. I plan to fly. I have a friend there and want to spend some time with her."

"We're going to stop at the Grand Canyon. My kids have always wanted to see that area."

I assured her that they would love it. "I've been there in summer and in winter, and it's always beautiful." I had another thought. "Do you have time to visit Sedona? The rock formations are spectacular, and it's not too far from the Grand Canyon."

She was tempted, I could see. "I need to talk to Tony and Thu. We have considered renting a van and all driving together. There will be seven of us."

"Is anyone coming from Vietnam?" I asked her.

Cam beamed, "Yes, my godmother and my husband's grandfather. Also my aunt and uncle from

Canada. Nieces and nephews will come from several US cities. There will be more than 30 people, I think."

Chapter 18

Lien's Story

The ship docked at Clark Air Force Base in the Philippines. We all lined up quietly and were served orange juice and cold drinks. Uniformed men and women offered sandwiches cut into four diamond shaped pieces. Many Vietnamese stuffed themselves and were nauseous. I only nibbled. I was too tired to eat much. The ones who had been sick were hungry a few hours later, but there was nowhere to buy food and no money to pay for it. All the gold had been sold to the Americans who worked on the Fleet ship.

We stayed in the barracks for two nights, and then re-boarded the ship, heading for Guam.

We spent the next few days on Guam, sleeping on cots in tents. It was windy, so our eyes stung with the sand blowing around inside the tents. My second brother-in-law's family joined us in Guam. I was happy to be on land, even though it was a sand pile.

The first morning we roused ourselves from our tent, three-year-old Dai followed his cousins' example of taking off his clothes. While the older children were splashing each other in the water fountain near our tent,

Dai picked up someone's discarded belt and fastened it around his naked belly, looking very pleased.

One of the other mothers approached me, holding her tiny daughter, and asked how we had slept in the tent. She looked exhausted. As soon as I responded, I turned back to Dai. He had disappeared. I tore around the area calling his name. No response. I ran back to the fountain and asked my nephews and nieces to help me look for him. We couldn't find him.

I was frantic. There were hundreds of children in the refugee camp, many of them naked. I stopped an officer and asked where I could get help to find my son. He kindly led me to the information office where I gave a description of Dai. The technician pulled the microphone close to his mouth and announced first in English, then in Vietnamese: "Now hear this. Now hear this. A three-year-old Vietnamese boy named Dai is missing. He is naked except for a large leather belt worn around his belly. If you see this boy, bring him to the information office immediately."

Within ten minutes Dai and I were reunited. The officer grinned, "Dai, you're a smart boy to wear a belt. Seems like that's the only way we could pick you out from the hundreds of kids here in the camp. Now stay near your mother, do you hear me?"

Dai nodded solemnly and wrapped his little arms tightly around my neck. He didn't have the words to tell me where he had been.

We flew from Guam to Fort Smith, Arkansas. Most families lived in refugee camps for no longer than three weeks before sponsors were located, and the families were flown to their new homes. Since our family was so large, we had to wait for sponsorship. Our family totaled 10.5 people. My baby was nearly ready to join us, and my pregnancy added to our delayed sponsorship.

Two weeks later, Quan and his wife returned. My sister-in-law felt well again. Their children were thrilled to see their parents. I was relieved to have part of my family with me again, but I badly missed Van.

I handed over the precious jacket to Quan, gold fully intact. He thanked me profusely.

I encouraged my two brothers-in-law to go ahead and not wait for my baby to be born, and we agreed that creating two smaller families might expedite finding sponsors. My second brother-in-law and his family immediately found a sponsor in Minneapolis and left Fort Smith. Quan refused to leave me on my own. I was grateful for this decision, especially with my baby's birth coming soon. Who would care for Dai while I was in labor?

I sold my last piece of gold jewelry to buy a coffee pot which I used to boil hot water for noodles. As soon as word spread through camp that someone could cook noodles, families were continually borrowing my pot. We all missed our native food. When the menu featured chicken, everyone was happy. The opposite was true when they served fish. Vietnamese prepare fish very differently than Americans. We like salty food, especially potato chips. Lots of gold jewelry was sold to supply Vietnamese families with potato chips.

I felt so alone on my own. Every night I would sit outside, gazing at the sky and crying. Why did I leave home? Where is my husband? What am I doing in a refugee camp about to have a baby all by myself?

A week after Quan and his wife returned, I felt the first contraction. It was followed by a stream of water running between my legs. I called the paramedics, who called for an ambulance. While I waited for the ambulance, my sister-in-law hovered around, but didn't come near me. She was chatting about my hospital suitcase, asking if I'd packed a tooth brush, robe, and hair brush. I was counting the seconds between contractions and wishing that Van was holding my hand.

Ten minutes later, I was strapped on a gurney. The medic asked my sister-in-law if she was going to ride with us. She shook her head, averting his eyes. She bent over me and whispered, "There are spirits of dead people in the ambulance. I cannot ride in it." The medics slammed the doors, and I was off to the hospital, alone.

She arrived at the hospital a few minutes after I had been admitted. The doctor assigned to me spoke French, as did my sister-in-law. My contractions were only seconds apart and I felt the baby moving lower. I spread my legs and started to push.

The doctor said something. My sister-in-law translated: "push." As if I needed an interpreter at this moment! I understood my job clearly and wished

135

fervently that she would stop speaking French and grab my hand instead. That didn't happen.

Very soon Bao was born, 7.5 pounds of her and all American. She was healthy and furious. I was elated, but began to cry immediately when I thought that her father had no idea he had a daughter.

I stayed in the hospital for two days. The second day, the nurse had me walking around trailing the IV. My arm was bleeding from the needle. I asked for a wheelchair, and the nurse laughed, thinking I was joking. I missed Dai, but hospital rules forbade children's visits.

When Dai was born in Vietnam, I stayed in the hospital for one month. I was instructed not to leave my bed. My mother practically moved in with me in case the nurses weren't giving me enough attention. I had to sneak out of bed to test my legs during the few minutes when both my mother and the nurses were out of the room. What a contrast to Bao's birth!

Chapter 19

Pasadena

Pasadena would be hot during the reunion, so I packed lightly. My Cal Tech friends, Lou and Sally, suggested I bring tennis shoes because they wanted to teach me their new favorite sport, pickleball. We had played tennis together in school years ago, and they promised I'd learn pickleball in 30 minutes. Why not? Despite faithfully paying gym fees, I was often too tired to exercise. Pickleball, whatever it was, might be just what I needed.

Lou and Sally were there to meet me at the Burbank airport two days before the reunion. It was great to see them and realize how little they had changed. I wished it were the same for me, but the lines around my mouth and eyes were a dead giveaway that twenty years and middle school children had made an impact on my face. Thank heaven I still wore the same size clothes, although I'd graduated to one shoe size larger. I was on my feet for hours in the classroom.

Their guest cottage was perfect and included a mini-kitchen so I could fix my own breakfast. I was glad I'd decided to stay with them. Olive trees and gigantic camellia bushes provided a shady setting behind their

Monterey-style house two blocks from Cal Tech. Sally told me I could walk to Lake Avenue and shop or grab a quick bite.

The next morning, Sal grinned as she handed me an oversized ping pong paddle. "Here's your weapon." Lou explained the rules which were just like old fashioned volley ball, with one additional score. As soon as I held the light paddle and bounced the whiffle ball on it, I wanted to find a court.

There were at least 25 people assembled on a tennis court converted to four smaller courts, all in use. I noticed right away how much fun people were having, laughing at each other and themselves. I had a very different memory of playing league tennis where all the women were serious, and teams wore matching outfits. Pickleball players apparently followed no dress codes.

After 20 minutes I was hooked. And tired. I wanted to have Tran, Tony and Thu play with me if there was time. Lou said they would be welcome anytime. There were plenty of loaner paddles and balls.

After we showered, Sal suggested we grab lunch at one of her favorite get-aways in Pasadena, the Norton Simon Museum. She promised a lovely garden atmosphere and a fresh salad. "Sounds great," I agreed.

We hadn't had a chance to really talk since my arrival. Although it had been several years since we'd seen each other, we kept in touch by phone. I guessed she wanted to ask about my divorce, since that was the major event since our last visit.

I explained to her that my marriage ended because Paul and I disagreed about having children. I had assumed we would have a family eventually. He insisted he'd never planned to have them.

It wasn't an issue while we were both paying off student loans. But when I turned 30, my loans were settled, we were both working, and I knew it was time. Paul thought we should use our money to invest for our retirement.

He bought himself a Ferrari for his 35th birthday and joined a car club. He spent most weekends on drives with his new buddies. I stayed home grading papers and developing lesson plans.

We lived in the same house but seemed to have forgotten why we had gotten married. No one was surprised when we ended the marriage. The divorce was not contentious. He accepted a job in Chicago. I hadn't seen him since he moved. But I clearly remember the day he left, feeling like I'd just missed the last train.

I explained to Sal that I had recently considered adopting a child but realized a single, working mother couldn't offer much to a baby who had already been abandoned once. And at 40, I didn't have the profile that agencies were seeking. So I fulfilled my maternal instincts with my students. It had worked well, not perfectly, but well enough. Dredging up these memories felt like running my tongue over a broken tooth.

Sal looked sympathetic and held my hand for a moment. There was nothing to say. She and Lou had two very attractive teenagers whom she thoughtfully didn't boast about.

I was tempted to tell her about missing the sound of Paul arriving home from work, the click of the door handle that now remained silent. About desolate Sunday mornings by myself, instead of sharing the newspaper in bed, Paul drinking coffee, me sipping tea. I even missed the little hairs in the sink when Paul trimmed his sideburns. I didn't want to dredge up my self-pitying miseries and the long tunnel of loneliness I'd been walking through. What good would it do?

*****

The reunion was to be held in a meeting room at the Hilton. Dinner that night was the official opening event. I suddenly felt nervous as I got dressed. All the questions I'd asked Tony, Thu and Cam re-surfaced. Would an outsider, a non-Vietnamese woman be welcome? What if the family preferred speaking Vietnamese? And so on. I shook my head, slipped on my sandals, straightened my skirt and told myself I didn't come all the way to California to get cold feet.

Tony picked me up in the van at exactly 6:00, as we had arranged. He looked fit and was impeccably dressed, as usual. "How was the Grand Canyon?" I asked after our greeting.

"Beautiful. Absolutely beautiful and massive. We loved it."

"Did you get to Sedona?"

"Unfortunately, we didn't have time. But I'd like to see it one day."

I asked him, "Did you do the driving?"

"Most of it, but Cam helped when I got tired. It was a fine trip." We were quiet for a minute. An awkward silence. Tony broke it. "You look very nice."

"Thank you," I replied.

"I wished you had driven with us."

I didn't know how to respond. I swallowed a tiny bubble of hope and simply said, "Thank you" again.

"Maybe we could take another driving trip to Sedona."

I glanced at him, but he was studiously facing forward. "That's a good idea." I hoped I sounded normal, but my stomach took a small leap.

Tony smiled and seemed to relax. He said quietly, turning toward me, "I have missed you."

Now my stomach lurched. Before thinking, I said, "I've missed you, too." He reached over and took my hand. I smiled at him and thought how good and natural his fingers felt, intertwined with mine.

Chapter 20

The Reunion

The party room at the Hilton was festive with Vietnamese and US flags. Bouquets of roses, dahlias, fuchsias and something aromatic, maybe jasmine, decorated each of the seven or eight tables. And the buffet! Never, never have I seen so much food. Cam's writing prize party was a mere introduction to this assortment of platters – noodles, rice, vegetables, fish, chicken, fruit, and many dishes completely foreign to me. The spicy aromas made my mouth water.

Cam pounced as soon as Tony and I entered the room. She took my arm. "We're going to start introductions with the elders. Just smile, that's all you have to do." I smiled and followed her.

Young men and women were talking earnestly at a few tables, with toddlers and kindergartners underfoot. All speaking English. Cam walked past them toward a table of older people, some who looked ancient, sitting quietly speaking Vietnamese together. That's where we were headed.

Cam introduced me to Grandfather from Saigon, who stood politely as we approached, leaning heavily on a cane. He was wizened, his left hand a curled nest. He was missing several teeth but managed a lopsided smile. He apparently spoke no English. His daughter, May, a puddle of a woman, was by his side and explained who I was.

The next couple were probably in their sixties, Vi and William Nguyen. Their expensive, tasteful outfits contrasted sharply with the baggy pants and wispy-haired older men with their wives, hunched but still sporting shoe-polish black hair. One wrinkled woman wore something that looked to me like pajamas.

Vi welcomed me with perfect, heavily accented British English and explained that she and William divided their time between Saigon and Los Angeles. I made a mental note to ask Tony about them. The others at the table were aunts, uncles and great-aunts and great-uncles. Cam explained that she had many people to introduce me to and guided me away.

As we headed for the next group, Cam grabbed the arm of a girl flying past, following two older children. "Tamara, slow down. I want you to say hello to Miss O'Neil." Tamara's eyes shone like dark crystal stones. She stopped immediately and held out her hand, "I'm very happy to see you again, Miss O'Neil." What lovely manners. I shook her hand.

"It's my pleasure, Tamara. Are you having fun at the reunion?"

"Yes, I am having a good time with my cousins. I don't see them very often," she added gravely.

"How about your uncles and aunts and grandparents?"

Her brows furrowed, then she thoughtfully replied, "I like most of them a lot, but I try to hide from Grandfather."

Cam and I both laughed at her candor. Cam didn't scold her, just patted her head and gave her permission to re-join the gang. Tamara hurled herself out of the room, chasing her cousins.

"What an adorable child, Cam." She was pleased with my praise.

"My son, William, is as serious as Tamara is happy-go-lucky."

"Well, you wouldn't want them to be the same, right?" Cam nodded her reply. "I'm looking for my husband, but I guess we'll catch up with him later."

Cam had done a good job in preparing her family for me. One after another thanked me for helping Vietnamese people learn English.

I finally spotted Tran hanging out with his cousins and went to say hello. He surprised me with a shy hug, then stepped quickly away. He politely introduced me to his cousins, all native English speakers.

I said to him, "Tran, I tried a new sport yesterday called pickleball." He made a face that indicated that pickles weren't on his list of favorite foods.

"I know it sounds weird, but it was really fun. You play it on a smaller tennis court. The friends I'm staying with have extra paddles and balls. Would you like to try it if we have time?"

Tran, always serious, answered, "Yes. I like games. As long as you don't have to be big to play them."

"I think small people are often faster, so you'll probably be good at it."

"Can my cousins come, too?"

"Of course, we can play doubles. The courts aren't far from here. Maybe there'll be time tomorrow."

Tran ran off in search of Thu and Tony. He was back right away looking excited. "Thu and Tony want to play, too. They said that tomorrow morning nothing is scheduled. Maybe some of the other cousins can come, too."

"Then it's a date."

Cam pulled me away for more introductions, followed by a huge meal, although I tried to sample only the unfamiliar dishes. Most were delicious.

After dinner, Cam looked expectant as she introduced me to her cousin, Thao, a slender, middle-aged man in beautifully tailored black slacks and a vanilla colored cashmere sweater draped casually over a slate gray shirt. "I think you and Thao have a lot in common. You are both very dedicated people."

She led us to an empty table and motioned for us to sit. We stared at each other for an awkward moment, then I asked Thao about his job. Cam slipped away.

"I'm an anesthesiologist at UCLA Medical Center." Thao's English was excellent. His quiet intensity made me want him beside me if I were undergoing surgery.

I asked him how he came to the US. Before he answered my question, he asked how I knew Cam. When I explained that Cam was in my advanced writing class, he nodded and smiled. "You're the one behind my cousin's obsession to write her memoirs, aren't you?"

I admitted that he was right, that Cam had begun by writing essays about her life as short homework assignments, then launched into a full autobiography.

Thao smiled, "Now I understand why she wanted us to talk. She has always encouraged me to write my own story, but I've never had the time or inspiration to do it." He paused, then looked directly at me. "But I will tell you my story, if you're interested."

"Absolutely," I assured him.

Chapter 21
Thao's Story

I was born in South Vietnam. My father was a French language professor and head of the language department at the university. My mother was a home-maker. They lived a privileged life before the war.

Most of our family escaped soon after the Fall, but my parents waited to observe the outcome of the war before fleeing the country. They had a lot to lose, but their lives disintegrated rapidly under the communists. They knew they should have left when the rest of the family escaped in 1975.

He faltered and looked away, sunk in memory. Anguish flashed in his eyes.

I can't describe the misery of our lives under the communists, but those of us who lived under their rule will never be the same. My parents included.

He paused again and regained his composure.

We spent five years trying to escape and finally obtained passage through Indonesia, Malaysia, Singapore, Thailand and China. We ended up in Guam where we lived in a refugee camp for many months. Too many months, according to my mother who still suffers nightmares about that experience.

At that time, first world countries were accepting Vietnamese refugees. My parents' first choice was Australia where my two uncles had settled. Our second choice was America. But the lottery system did not work in our favor. We received sponsorship in Canada, our third choice.

A Catholic church in Montreal sponsored our family. The church members found jobs for my parents and rented us a home in a small rural town. My father's graduate degrees from Vietnam did not transfer to Canada, and Montreal was French-speaking, so he couldn't find a teaching position.

After two difficult, lonely years working as a janitor and taking English classes at night, my father heard there were job opportunities and a better life out west. He could only afford one bus fare to Vancouver.

After nine months, he saved enough from his factory job to send bus tickets to my mother and me. The factory was owned by a South Vietnamese family. My mother immediately found a job in a restaurant not far from our apartment and worked long hours.

We shared a rundown apartment with another Vietnamese family. There were five adults and three children in that tiny space. The children's aunt slept in a closet. Our family slept in the living room; and the other parents and two children slept in the bedroom.

All the adults found jobs, some in the day, others at night. The children from the other family watched over me. I played with other immigrant kids in our building. There were no nannies and no pre-school.

The year I started first grade, my parents made a down payment on a small house. We were all so happy to be living in our own space. No aunties sleeping in the closet. I had my own small bedroom and experienced privacy for the first time in my life.

I will never forget my dad walking me to my first day of school. He tied a house key around my neck, gave me a pat on the head, told me to be a good student, and shoved me gently toward the door. He turned and left me there. I was terrified. No one but the teacher spoke to me for many weeks.

The walk home that first day seemed so far, although it really wasn't. I watched carefully for the signposts I'd noticed on the way that morning. Turn left at the corner with the blue house. Walk two more blocks. Cross the street where the fruit stand was. Then one more block to our house. I used my key to enter our silent house and waited for my parents to come home. We didn't have a TV.

From that day on, I walked by myself to and from school. No one was ever home when I unlocked the door. I watched the kitchen clock while I did my homework until it said five. Then my dad usually came home.

I became a responsible person that first day of school, and those experiences shaped me into the person

I am today. My own son is now six. I can't imagine him being responsible for himself or alone in the house, nor would I want him to be. I learned later in life that I was a "latch key" kid. I didn't know that other kids lived differently. I thought I was living a normal Canadian childhood. I didn't know what a latch key was.

My parents insisted on speaking Vietnamese at home because English was my first language. They wanted me to keep our heritage. My father was very displeased if I spoke English.

My baby brother was born when I was in second grade, and then my sister a year later. At nine years old, I picked them up from day care, fed them, and cared for them till my mom or dad returned from work. My sense of responsibility tripled when my siblings became my job. I've worked hard all my life and even today have trouble doing something just for fun.

My parents continued to work long hours and saved enough money for my mom to buy a small coffee shop. I worked there every weekend, sweeping floors, baking cookies, washing dishes – anything that had to be done.

There was no time to play with other kids. I led a Vietnamese life in Canada.

I remember one Saturday walking home with my mom after working in the cafe. Her purse was heavy with money. We sat at the kitchen table and counted it together. I felt proud that I had helped earn that money.

A few years later, my dad bought a franchise for a chain restaurant. Both my parents worked so hard they weren't even home on the weekends. Getting the kids fed, bathed, and homework done all fell to me. My siblings and I didn't receive any guidance from our parents. We were hardly connected to them emotionally. My brother and sister spoke only English.

When I wasn't doing housework or homework, I remember staring out the window, wishing I were a normal kid. I day-dreamed that my mom handed me my lunch box with a secret smile as she walked me to school. When lunchtime came, I would find she had made my favorite chocolate pudding as a surprise.

We were the only Vietnamese students at our Catholic school, but there were lots of Filipino kids who became our friends and still are. We had some white friends, but kids tend to gravitate toward others like themselves.

As a teenager, I had no chance to be rebellious. But my sister and brother were considerably younger and truly Canadian. They didn't have the same work ethic my parents and I shared. I went away to college. They rebelled.

When I left for college, my sister and brother were completely unsupervised. They began to run with the wrong crowd, experiment with drugs, and ignore their school work. I wasn't there to stop them. When my parents were called to the principal's office to discuss their children's failing grades, they were shocked and horrified. They asked themselves where they had been all these years.

151

My parents woke up and sold their businesses. They told my siblings that they were there for them. That an education was important. That they needed to go to college. Their futures were why they left Vietnam. But it was too late. It took my brother and sister many years to "find themselves," as Americans say. But eventually they finished school and became professionals. My brother is a nurse, and my sister is a geologist.

Thao bowed his head and stopped talking for a minute. He breathed deeply and continued.

"My wife and I face the same challenges as my parents did – struggling to make a good living and still raising our family. We have a daughter and a son. We're trying to keep our Vietnamese traditions alive, which isn't easy in a North American world."

He closed his eyes for a moment.

I went to medical school at UCLA and never returned to Canada. I became a US citizen. My parents are still in Vancouver. We see them on holidays."

I wanted to understand more about this complex, sensitive, intelligent man. "Please tell me about living a mixed cultural life."

Thao knitted his eyebrows and thought before he responded.

"I want my children to speak Vietnamese and to visit Vietnam. I want them to work hard and respect their elders. I want them to value education and strive to do the best they can in all phases of their lives."

He paused. "But I also want them to have fun and be silly and go to Disneyland. I'm actually not certain how to do this. But I know one thing for sure. My wife and I need to spend as much time with them as we can. We have promised each other not to raise latch key children."

I replied, "Thao, my experience as a teacher of middle school children is that most of the troubled kids suffer from a poor home life. Their parents are simply too busy to know what's going on with their kids. I can't imagine that happening in your home."

Thao still looked concerned. "I'm basically a workaholic. So is my wife. Since I'm in the medical field, I'm called away at all hours. It's extremely difficult to say no when I'm called for an emergency."

"Does your wife need to travel for her job?"

"Sometimes, but we're fortunate that she reports to a woman who seems to understand that Vanessa needs to be home at night."

"Is your wife Vietnamese?"

"No, she's black."

I knew Thao's story wasn't finished, but his son rushed up and begged to go swimming. Thao hugged the boy, brown as a nut, and excused himself.

I really wanted to hear the rest of this story of two cultures. I hoped we'd have another chance to talk. I wanted to ask him whether his wife's family accepted her marrying an Asian and how his family reacted to their marriage. "Thao, I'd like to hear more about your family. Would it be Okay if we talked later?"

He nodded gravely, "Certainly. I'll be here for two more days. I'm sorry my wife couldn't get away from work. I think you two would enjoy each other."

Chapter 22

Uncle Ba

After breakfast the next day, Cam was waiting at the Hilton for me. She and I joined the circle of family members who sat listening to an older man speaking Vietnamese. He gestured angrily with both gnarled hands, spitting as he spoke. Tony slid onto the chair next to me and whispered. "This is Uncle Ba who lives in San Jose. He escaped from Saigon after the Tet Offensive. He's talking about his life. Would you like me to translate?" Of course I wanted to know what the tirade was about. I nodded yes.

I lost everything when I came to this country. I was a doctor, but my certifications meant nothing here. I had a big house in Saigon, a driver, a cook, and a maid. My wife never had to do housework. My sons went to the best schools.

When Saigon fell to the communists, we escaped by boat. Several people died during the passage. We ran out of food before the navy picked us up. Some of the people ate the flesh of the dead men. My family and I did not. We would rather die.

When we were rescued, we were sent to a camp in the Philippines where we waited for three months for a sponsor. I tried to help other refugees when they became ill, but I couldn't obtain the proper medicine because I couldn't communicate with the American medical staff.

The US government finally flew us to Los Angeles, then to San Jose. We did not speak English. Our French was useless.

Uncle Ba paused for a moment, his mouth a grimace, his eyes tortured. No one said a word. Tony laid his hand on my arm and whispered, "He isn't finished yet." I wondered how he knew.

The church that sponsored us rented us an apartment. They said I had to get a job. We had some gold, but not enough.

My wife and I both worked as janitors at a bad motel in San Jose. My wife had never cleaned a toilet in her life. Neither had I. The church people took us to English classes, but we couldn't learn quickly. After a few months, we learned, but Americans couldn't understand us. They yelled at us to speak English, even though we were trying to speak English to them.

My sons learned English quickly and adjusted to this country. My wife and I did not. We now live with my eldest son in San Jose. I spend the days talking to my Vietnamese friends, smoking and drinking iced coffee.

My wife watches Vietnamese films she gets at the library. We watch TV at night.

My dream is to return to Saigon and reclaim my home. The communists will not allow this. I will die in a foreign country.

He seemed exhausted when he finished. I assumed from the neutral faces of the listeners that he had told this story before. They were showing respect by listening. Tony confirmed my assumption.

He motioned me to follow him outside to the balcony where he explained, "There are many older people like Uncle who are bitter. They have never adjusted to this country. They spend their days dreaming of the past, telling old stories, and hating the communists. It is a sad way to end life."

I responded, "It's difficult for me to understand, since I have no experience as an ex-pat. I'm sorry for him, Tony." Tony merely nodded. After a moment, I asked him, "What is the difference between people like your uncle and you and Thu?"

"What do you mean?"

I explained, "You and Thu have learned English. You have a job. You don't talk about the old days. You look to the future."

"I understand your question," he replied. He thought before answering. "I am proud to be an American. I can make my life a success if I work hard. I have choices.

Uncle and many of the others could not start over again, for many reasons. I think he is a proud man and couldn't start a new life here. He was very successful in Saigon."

"So it's more about each person than a national issue. Is that what you're saying?"

"Yes, if you visit San Jose, for example, you will find angry people like Uncle Ba living a Vietnamese life. But you will also find people like Thu and me living American lives. I think we are happier."

Then he added, "Language is a huge hurdle for older Vietnamese. Even though they take English classes, Americans can't understand them because of their heavy accents. This makes them very angry. They were used to giving orders in Vietnam and never being questioned. Now, they can't even order in a restaurant and be understood. I've seen Uncle Ba point to an item on a menu rather than risk being misunderstood."

"Tony, I've never seen this kind of anger when I teach ESL. I've observed my students' frustration and fear, but never this level of bitterness."

"Callie, you haven't been teaching elderly Vietnamese people who have lost their country."

We were both quiet for a moment. I asked myself what made him so different from many of his family members, I knew he worked in a factory, but that's all I knew. He had hinted during one of our Sunday writing lessons that he had thought about another profession, but we'd never returned to this topic.

"Tony, when we have some quiet time, will you tell me your plans?"

"My plans?" He looked perplexed.

"Your dreams about the future."

I was rewarded by his grin. "Of course. We'll need at least an hour. I have many plans." He took my hand between both of his and winked at me. Winked! I'd never seen Tony wink. I wondered if this was a Vietnamese gesture, but guessed it wasn't. My stomach fluttered.

Cam stuck her head around the door to the balcony, glanced at Tony and me holding hands, but her face betrayed nothing. "Are you ready for more introductions?" I pulled my hand free. Cam was taking her care-giver role very seriously. "Of course. Who's next?"

Instead of answering, she asked, "What did you think about Uncle Ba?"

I wasn't sure how to respond but decided to be honest. "He makes me very sad. I feel that the US has let him down somehow. I'm sorry he's so unhappy.

Cam replied, "He and his cronies are sad, understandable when you think about how much they have lost. They never stop dreaming about going back to Vietnam. So, in some way, they won't allow themselves to be happy."

I said, "It's complicated, Cam, isn't it? What would happen if they returned for a visit?"

"I think you should ask Uncle Ba. I would be interested in his answer, too. Maybe you can talk to him later. But now, I have something else in mind." She took my hand and guided me to a group of young adults. Before we reached the group, Cam lowered her voice.

"Those are my nieces and nephews. They were all born in America or Canada. I'd like you to meet my favorite niece, Sherry. That's the name she chose for herself." She pointed to a petite girl sporting a magenta crop top and jeans. Her long black hair was pulled into a pony tail. Her face was lovely.

Cam cleared her throat, "I want you all to meet my English teacher, Miss O'Neil. This is Sherry, Robert, Wayne, Kate and Andrew." They were polite, apparently waiting for Cam to say something, but she didn't.

Sherry broke the awkward silence, "Cam has told me so much about you, Miss O'Neil." She smiled at me with Hollywood-quality white teeth. I'm so pleased to meet you." I shook her outstretched hand.

"I'm happy to meet you too, Sherry." The others seemed to relax, and one by one, we shook hands. But I felt that a group conversation wasn't going to happen. I turned to Sherry, "Can I tear you away for a few minutes? Cam says you are a very interesting young woman." Sherry blushed, making her prettier than ever.

"Would you like to take a walk?" she suggested.

"Great idea." We left the party room and headed for the hotel lobby. Sherry knew where she was going. "Let's walk to Old Town. Have you been there?"

"No, my hostess said we'd have dinner there one night, but I'd love to see it."

We walked in companionable silence for a few moments.

Sherry turned toward me. "I think Aunt Cam wanted us to meet because I told her about my brother Dan's problem." She frowned.

"Did I meet your brother?"

"He was the one in the black tee shirt, with the nose ring."

"Oh yes, I noticed him, but we weren't introduced. I don't know if I met your parents either."

"Their American names are Will and Katherine. They were sitting with Grandfather."

"I'm not sure. Anyway, tell me about your brother."

Sherry took a deep breath. "Okay, Dan and my parents aren't getting along."

"Why not?" I asked.

"He's just not doing what they want."

"Tell me more."

Sherry sighed, "My parents want Dan to be a doctor. They say that doctors will always have a job. But Dan wants to be a filmmaker. They don't even know what a filmmaker does. And they don't want to know."

I remembered reading accounts of immigrant youth arguing with their parents over expectations they didn't share. "I'm sorry, Sherry, this must make things difficult for all of you. Are you and Dan close?"

"Yes, we are. As close as I can be to someone who's always angry." Sherry grimaced. "It's like I'm the favorite child because I get good grades, and believe it or not, I want to be a pediatrician."

I had to smile at the irony of the daughter following the path designed for the son. Sherry continued quickly, pouring out her feelings. "I'm always sticking up for Dan, but it doesn't help. My parents are very traditional. They expect the oldest son to be respectful and take care of them in their old age. They don't think a filmmaker will be about to do that."

I interjected, "Who knows, Dan may be a millionaire."

Sherry wrinkled her nose. "Not likely. His grades are terrible. And his friends aren't the best. They mostly hang out, drink beer and who knows what else."

I tried to be optimistic. "Well, artists aren't known to be great students. They march to a different drummer."

Sherry did not appear to have heard me, or at least not to agree with my observation. "You probably don't understand Vietnamese families. The ones whose parents were boat people."

"I'd like you to explain it to me. I teach English to Vietnamese adults and would like to understand them better."

Sherry spoke very quickly. "Okay. My parents sacrificed everything when they left their country. My father was a history professor. He had the equivalent of a Master's degree. My mother never worked. When they came here, they had nothing. My father used to be important in the community. When they came to California, they couldn't even speak English."

This was a story I was becoming very familiar with. My heart went out to these brave people who had to start life again, sometimes in middle-age. Sherry interrupted my thoughts.

"Dan is very American. He says what he thinks and doesn't listen to my parents. I'm caught in the middle. I try to be respectful to my parents and a friend to Dan, but I can't fix their relationship. I've tried and tried." Sherry stopped walking and closed her eyes. I saw tears escaping down her cheeks. I put my arm gently around her shoulders. "Oh Sherry, you just have to be you. Dan is following his own path. It doesn't sound like he'll change. And your parents will continue suffering, but your love and your future will help them immensely. They'll be so proud of you."

Sherry's expression was grim as he wiped her tear away. "Do you know the term "tiger parents"?"

"I think it refers to Asian parents who push their children very hard."

She nodded, "That's right. I knew a boy who killed himself last year because he couldn't meet his parents' expectations."

I was horrified. "Do you worry about your brother doing something like that?"

She answered, "Yes, I did when he was younger. He used to shut himself in his room and refuse to come out. My parents hounded him about his poor grades. But I've stopped thinking he'd ever commit suicide."

"Why?" I asked.

"Because lately he's just rebellious. He's given up on pleasing my parents, which is a good and a bad thing. It's good because I think he's safe, but bad because my parents and grandparents are so disappointed."

Then I had a strange thought. "I think you'll end up being the eldest son!"

Sherry looked at me in amazement. "Miss O'Neil, I've never thought about it like that. I can be the oldest son!" Her face was radiant as she did a little dance, then spontaneously gave me a hug and swung me in a circle. Her words poured out: "You don't know how much you've helped me. I can't explain why. Just let me say how grateful I am."

I didn't understand her elation, but was delighted I was somehow part of it.

We'd arrived in the busy Old Town area of Pasadena. Sherry's whole demeanor had changed from a worried teen to a happy, excited young woman. She beamed, "Let's celebrate. Here's one of my favorite coffee houses." We ordered, and she grabbed the check. "My treat. In America, girls are allowed to pay the bill." She gave me a wicked smile.

Chapter 23

Pickleball on Day Three of the Reunion

Try to picture twelve Vietnamese people ranging from 10 to 45 years old, swatting whiffle balls across a low tennis net. Two older women wore long skirts, reminding me of sepia photos of early female tennis champions. The men wore long pants. Only the young people looked natural in shorts.

Tony appeared to be very serious about learning the rules and techniques. Sal, my hostess, turned out to be a great instructor, and soon Tony was exchanging long rallies with her. Thu did a lot of swinging and missing, but seemed to be having fun. For the first time since I'd met her, she was laughing outright without covering her crooked teeth with her hand.

The surprise was Tran! He loved the game. His blade-thin legs flew around the court. He swooped like a fish in water. Although he was small, he was able to smash overheads with amazing strength and accuracy. He won every game, regardless of his partner's skills. I recognized the look of someone who has fallen in love.

When we finally left the courts to get ready for lunch at the reunion, Tran had a Christmas morning look when he asked me, "Miss O'Neil, do you think we could play pickleball in PE?"

"Well, I know Mr. Thomas pretty well. I could certainly ask him. Do you think your friends would like it?"

Tran's face fell, "I don't really have many friends." I was sorry for blundering.

"You know, Tran, pickleball might just be the way you'll make some friends. You're really a natural at it. I bet you could sort of be the leader in getting it going."

Tran couldn't hide his excitement. He squirmed with happiness. I wasn't sure if it was about finding friends or playing pickleball. Maybe it was both.

*****

We were back at the Hilton for lunch after pickleball. I found Sherry and asked her to introduce me to her parents, which she graciously did. I sat down at their table and told them how much I had enjoyed their daughter's company the day before. They were all smiles until I asked about Dan. Then both faces clouded, displaying years of disappointment.

Sherry's father answered sternly. "Dan is difficult. He is not a good student." I waited for more. His wife added. "We worry that Dan will not be successful. He

167

will not earn enough money to buy a car or go to college."

I tried to be compassionate. "Well, some young people have to find their own way. Dan may have talents outside of school. He may find a wonderful career doing something he loves." I paused, knowing they didn't believe me. I added lamely, "I know this must be difficult for you."

The parents exchanged a look. The father said, "We worry about our son."

I was relieved when Tony joined us and asked softly, "Callie, may I speak to you for a minute?"

I was grateful for an excuse to end this conversation. "I'll see you later," I told the sad couple as I walked away with Tony.

He asked, "What was that about? All three of you looked so serious."

"I was saying how much I enjoyed talking to Sherry. And then they told me how worried they were about Dan."

"Yes," he sighed, "We all know about Dan. But not all of us worry."

I was curious about his remark. "What do you mean?"

"Let's sit down over there for a minute, at that empty table." I followed him to a deserted table in the corner. Tony lowered his voice. "Dan is very bright. In fact, maybe brilliant."

My eyebrows shot up. "I'm listening." I leaned towards him so I could catch every word.

"He's an artist. He writes scripts, acts in school plays, draws portraits and is a serious reader."

I was amazed. "What's with his relationship with his parents?"

Tony sighed. "They don't want him to be anything but a doctor or an engineer. You can understand why. In Vietnam, artists aren't considered traditional professions."

"I see," I answered slowly. "How do you think this will turn out?" Before he could respond, I blurted, "Tony, yesterday I told Sherry that she might fill the role of older son."

He stared at me, then squinted. Finally, he leaned over and kissed my cheek. "You are brilliant."

"Please explain," I begged.

Tony thought again, apparently searching for the right words. His reaction mirrored Sherry's. "In Vietnamese culture, the eldest son's role is to support and care for his parents. He is expected to marry and bring his wife home to live in his parents' home. She becomes her mother-in-law's servant, or sort of servant. It depends." Tony noticed my dismay.

"Callie, I'm just explaining tradition. Not what I think or plan to do."

"Okay," I answered softly. "Please continue."

"It is extremely important for the eldest son to be a financial success since he'll be responsible for his parents and their home once his father retires."

"I understand. Now please tell me why you and Sherry reacted so strongly to my comment to her."

Tony beamed, "Because you have captured the difference in how life can change for Vietnamese people in America. There are options in this country that don't exist in Vietnam."

I must have looked as perplexed as I felt, so Tony continued. "By saying that Sherry could be the eldest son, you allowed her to take responsibility for her parents as they age. She plans to be a doctor. She knows she'll be able to afford care and housing for them. It doesn't have to be Dan's responsibility. Do you see?"

I was beginning to understand. The American paradigm could replace the pattern from the old country. Elders would be cared for, but not necessarily by the eldest son and not necessarily by moving into the parents' home. Sherry had immediately captured those possibilities once Dan was off the hook.

I smiled back at Tony. "It was a lucky guess, Tony. I have a lot to learn about your culture. To be honest, I can't imagine moving back to my mother's home. I would be more than willing to support her financially and emotionally, but I can't see myself giving up my independence." I heard how harsh this might have sounded to Tony, so I asked, "Tony, do you think I'm terrible?"

He took my hand. "No, I think you are honest and very American. That's why I like being with you."

Cam headed toward us. "Here you are. And I was worried that Miss O'Neil would be lonely! Not a chance, I see." But she looked at Tony approvingly.

"Cam, would you please call me Callie, at least outside the classroom."

"I would love to. Thank you so much. I think that means we are friends."

"That's exactly what it means," I assured her.

Chapter 24

Auntie Kim

Cam led me to a table of older family members. "Callie, I'd like you to meet my aunt who lives in Wisconsin. She has a very interesting life story that I think you'll want to hear." I couldn't help but wonder when Cam was going to run out of relatives I had to meet. But there was a method to her determination. I was certain of that. Tony nodded his concurrence and followed us to a table where the conversation was lively and in Vietnamese.

"Excuse me," Cam interrupted. "I'd like you to meet Miss Callie O'Neil. I have told you that she is my teacher. She is also interested in learning about our culture. I thought Auntie Kim might tell Callie her story."

A miniature porcelain peacock of a woman in a beautiful blue silk blouse and tailored black pants patted the chair beside her, inviting me to sit down. I smiled and sat.

I addressed Auntie Kim directly but included the others with my eyes when I said, "Did you know that Cam is writing her memoir?" Blank faces. I quickly added, "I meant to say that Cam is writing the story of her life. She started with her most important memories. I'm sure that many of you will be included in her book." Many smiles and nods of approval. Cam winked at me. "Cam is a very good writer," I added. Even broader smiles.

I turned to my seat-mate. "I am honored to meet you, Aunt Kim. And I'm very interested in hearing about your life." That was all she needed to hear. She straightened her back and began her monologue.

In fluent English, the delicate woman began in a reedy voice that grew stronger as she spoke.

After the fall of the south, my sister and other family members escaped from the communists as boat people. My husband and I also wanted to flee, but we knew we were being watched whenever we left the house together.

She raised a slim, ringed finger, and arched her carefully painted eyebrows.

Fine lines appeared on her smooth forehead.

We devised an ingenious escape plan. In broad daylight, my husband casually walked along the beach. He climbed aboard a fishing boat, greeting his friends and taking the pole they handed to him. The beach patrol didn't pay any attention since men did this daily.

There were 15 people on the boat when my husband climbed in. Thirty-five more joined them, hiding below. The group dangerously overloaded the boat as they headed out to sea.

The plan was to arrive in Hong Kong where a rescue ship was waiting, but a typhoon was coming, so they changed course and headed for the Philippines, hoping they would be rescued there.

Auntie Kim paused to explain to me that escapees had to go to the country where an assigned rescue ship was waiting. They couldn't just head for another country and expect sanctuary.

She continued her narrative, addressing the entire group, but making frequent eye contact with me. I guessed I was the only one unfamiliar with her story, but her family sat in rapt attention.

After several days at sea, the small overloaded boat was hit by a typhoon. They had not eaten is several days. Only two of the men were strong enough to lift buckets to bail the water that was sinking the boat. Many were seasick, others were simply too weak.

The waves overwhelmed the boat. The men threw everything they could into the sea to lighten the load. They wondered if they would survive. Many thought they would die and went below, accepting their fate. My husband was not ready to die. He joined the two other men above and began to bail.

A ship tried to rescue them, but couldn't come close enough because the waves were too powerful, and the boats would collide. After that failure, they were not scared anymore. They were ready to die.

Auntie Kim's voice was so low, I had to lean toward her to catch her next words.

When you escape from your country, you understand you may very well die.

She paused, wiped her lips delicately on a linen handkerchief and continued.

Finally, they saw a bird and were encouraged about reaching land. On the seventh day, they landed on an island where the inhabitants took them to a church and gave them food and water. They slept there for one night. While they slept, the islanders crept into the church and stole their valuables: watches, gold, whatever was left.

When their boat finally arrived in the Philippines, only three of the original 50 men were alive. The other two men ate the flesh of the dead. My husband decided he would rather die than be a cannibal. He suffered from nightmares for years and took sleeping pills until the night his heart gave out. But that was many years later.

He spent three years in the Philippines camp. Others were there for ten or more years. One of his friends told my husband that on his boat there were eleven people. They killed one man in order to eat. Another described seeing her three daughters drown at sea.

A man in my husband's camp had witnessed a Thai pirate gang punch a hole in an escapees' boat. The pirates climbed on board and raped a woman in front of her husband. The victim was so embarrassed she could not look at anyone. The man had tears in his eyes telling us this story. My husband knew the woman was his wife.

My husband learned English while he waited in the camp. When he wasn't studying, he tried to help the other refugees, making them laugh and singing to them. He loved music and was a natural actor. He sang in the camp's Catholic choir and also for the Buddhists.

Auntie Kim sighed deeply and took a long drink of iced tea. It appeared she was finished. I was so curious I couldn't help myself from blurting, "How did you become reunited?" She must have been waiting for me to ask because her words cascaded.

Before the war, all I heard was how wonderful it would be to live in the USA. I knew nothing about Canada. I was single then and taught high school biology. I met my husband when he joined the faculty at my school, and we were married a few months later. We began to make plans to escape together to California.

After my husband escaped without me, I was sent to an even poorer school in the country as punishment. I met a teacher there who was a good man and treated me like a sister. He was planning to escape and wanted me to leave with him and his family. He told me his plan about fixing up a boat at night when no one could see what he was doing.

My husband's parents didn't want me to go because they were afraid I would die. I told them I had to see my husband, their son, again. They finally agreed I could go if their daughter went with me. I told my teacher friend about my sister-in-law, but he said no, there was no room for another person. The boat could only hold 20 people, and not one more. I told him sadly that I couldn't go then without my sister-in-law.

The day of the escape, my teacher friend relented and said my sister-in-law could come. We followed my husband's plan and left as fishermen in daylight. The women were hiding below.

I was so seasick, I couldn't eat at all. I sucked on a piece of pineapple for the five days we were at sea. Nothing more. I was very weak.

Our boat had kind people onboard. But around the boat I saw terrible things happen. A man in our boat recognized a friend on a different boat. He jumped in the sea to swim to his friend, but he drowned. We threw him things to save him, but he disappeared in the sea.

My teacher friend said we would try to go to the Philippines. But a storm came up, so we had to go to Hong Kong along the coast. I didn't care. I just wanted to get on land. A second storm prevented us from landing in Hong Kong. We finally landed in Macau.

The United Nations people at the camp in Macau understood the hardships the South Vietnamese people had experienced and treated us well. The camp manager assigned us a safe place in the camp. Boat people from North Vietnam were treated harshly as if they were the enemy.

I spent three years in the Macau camp, waiting for my husband to find a country that would take him. The United Nations kept a list of who was in which camp, so I knew where my husband was. We wrote love letters. I have two shoe boxes of these letters in my closet.

My husband considered emigrating to England where his sister lived. His brother was in Canada. The UN officials advised him to go to Canada rather than England, since life was better there. He knew I wanted to live in the US, but we had no one to sponsor us. So my husband flew to Toronto and re-started his life there, thinking Canada was closer to California than England.

After three years of separation, I gave up my dream of California and flew to Toronto to join my husband. We became Canadian citizens. We had two daughters who are now grown. My husband died of a heart attack two years ago. I miss him very much.

Auntie Kim lowered her head, but not before I saw tears squeeze from her eyes. Her audience remained respectfully silent for a minute. She looked up and smiled weakly at me, then continued.

We started from nothing in Toronto. My husband got a job at the post office and worked there the rest of his life. I took in sewing and worked in a beauty parlor. We managed.

Every Sunday my husband taught Vietnamese to first generation Vietnamese/Canadian children so they could communicate with their grandparents and parents.

Auntie Kim seemed to be finished. I finally asked, "Do you still dream about living in California?"

She chuckled, "No, I have grandchildren in Toronto. And I visit my family here whenever it gets too cold. My life in Canada is good, especially the health care. I have no complaints."

I responded, "I wish I could have met your husband. He sounds like a generous, warm person."

"I wish that, too. You would have loved him. Everyone did." With that, she rose and excused herself. I think we were all exhausted from her tale. I was grateful she shared her memories so readily with me. I turned to Cam and thanked her for introducing me to this extraordinary woman.

Cam gave me her teasing look. "Auntie Kim didn't tell you her whole story."

"What did she leave out?" I was very curious.

Cam explained, "When she said she took in sewing, it seems one of her customers was a clothes designer. Auntie Kim became her assistant and had a wonderful career that included flying to Paris and New York for fashion shows."

I was astounded. "Why did she leave this out of her story?"

Cam was thoughtful. "I think she wanted to tell you her love story tonight. It wasn't the right time to talk about business."

Once again I realized how little I knew about Vietnamese culture! If I had told that story, my career as a fashion designer would have come first.

Chapter 25

Final Day of the Reunion

On the last day of the reunion, I got up early to meet Tony and Thu for breakfast by the pool. Tran was already swimming with his cousins. Tony and Thu were sitting under an umbrella talking to an attractive 30-ish Vietnamese woman whom I hadn't met.

They appeared to be having a lively discussion as I approached the table.

"Callie, I'd like you to meet Amber. She lives in the Bay Area." Tony pulled out a chair so I could join them.

They didn't resume their conversation, so I realized I'd interrupted something personal. "I'm sorry to have intruded. You obviously were talking about something important before I barged in. Let me join you in a few minutes." I got up to leave.

Amber motioned me to sit down. She sighed and asked, "Callie, Thu and Tony have told me you teach English to Vietnamese adults."

"That's right."

"Do most of them have children?" What was this about?

"Yes, I think all the Vietnamese women I've taught have children. Why do you ask?"

Another deep sigh and her brows furrowed. She was exceptionally pretty when she wasn't frowning. She wore designer jeans and a fashionable flowing emerald top.

"I was 30 last month, and my husband and I don't have children."

I had no idea how to respond. Was I supposed to say I'm sorry, or why not, or have you looked into fertility? So I said nothing.

"I was explaining to Tony and Thu that Steve and I want to have a family but we're afraid to."

Now I couldn't keep still. "Why, Amber?"

"Because of Steve's parents. My mother-in-law is a traditional Vietnamese mother and will be a traditional Vietnamese grandmother. Steve and I want to raise an American family, but my in-laws live in the house next door."

I knew I was supposed to understand her dilemma, but I didn't. I gave Thu a 'help me' look.

Thu explained that Vietnamese grandparents traditionally take care of the children while the parents work. They take care of them even if the mother stays home.

Amber's voice was rising, "I can't even trust my mother-in-law to take care of our dogs. If Steve and I go away for the weekend, she feeds the dogs from the table, as much as they'll eat. She says that the dry food I bring over isn't fit for a pig. Imagine what she'd do with a baby!"

I asked if she and Steve could move, even to another state. Amber had obviously thought of that. "My in-laws are retired and would follow wherever we live. Steve is the eldest son and is responsible for caring for his parents. We had to convince them to buy the house next door after I nearly lost my mind when they lived with us for the first two years after our marriage."

It was clear to me what Amber and Steve should do, but I doubted that my solution would be accepted culturally. I looked to the cousins for help. "Were you giving Amber some advice when I joined you?" Tony and Thu shook their heads. Thu answered, "No, we were telling Amber we were so sorry she and Steve didn't think it was time to start their family."

I couldn't bear it. The outspoken American jumped out of my mouth. "Amber, it seems to me that you and Steve have a difficult decision to make. Either forego having a family (Amber shuddered) or confront your in-laws."

Amber asked harshly, "What do you mean, confront your in-laws?"

Now I was in waist deep. "Well, I guess you'll have to explain to them that you intend to raise your children the American way. That your children will be very lucky to have their grandparents nearby to share their lives; but that you and Steve intend to determine what and when they eat and sleep, what they can and cannot do, and where they can and cannot go. This is the American way you intend to follow. And you hope they understand how much you love and respect them."

Amber looked devastated. In a small voice she said that she and Steve knew this, but they were afraid to confront his parents after all the older people had sacrificed for them.

"I'm sorry, Amber. I guess you and Steve are the only ones who can decide if and when you have this conversation with his parents."

Amber said bitterly as she got up from the table, "If we don't have this conversation soon, all we'll be able to raise is dogs." And she left, muttering something about her in-laws being like unsinkable old ships.

Tony grinned at me. "You are a tiger, Callie. Thu nodded in agreement.

*****

Cam and I managed to sit next to Uncle Ba at lunch. He was focusing on his full plate of food, but responded politely when I greeted him.

"May I call you Uncle Ba since everyone else does?" Cam translated.

His small black eyes twinkled, "I did not think I would ever have a niece who looks like you. But you may call me Uncle, if you like."

Phew! Now came the part I'd rehearsed that morning. "Have you visited Vietnam since leaving so many years ago?"

His face became a storm. His mouth narrowed to a slit. His lips disappeared. He slammed his chopsticks on the table, and his words came in a torrent. "I will never visit Vietnam while the communists run my country." His voice hung in the air like a smoggy day.

I wondered if I should leave it at that, but good sense deserted me, despite Cam's warning glance. "If you went back, do you think you would be safe?"

"Safe?" His face contorted. His double chins wobbled. He spat, "I would be safe, but I would be treated like dirt. Nothing has changed since the communists took over. Government officials would demand money to let me leave the airport. I would be harassed and spied on every minute. Why would I put myself in that position? I will never visit Vietnam until the communists leave."

I knew I had upset him, so I tried to shift the conversation to more neutral topics, then Cam and I excused ourselves. I was certain I had ruined his meal.

When we were out of ear shot, Cam explained that Uncle Ba and others who suffered under the communists were deeply, irrevocably scarred. I pictured lines of elderly Vietnamese people dragging their pasts stuffed in old, battered suitcases.

Then Cam surprised me by saying that she and her husband had visited Vietnam for a wedding three years ago. They stayed at her uncle's home, who owned many acres of land. After lunch on the day they arrived, she asked to use the toilet. Her uncle's servant led her to a man-made pond in front of the house filled with gigantic koi fish. The house was directly behind the pond. There was a raised wood structure over the pond with a hole for a toilet. The koi ate the human waste.

Cam saw my astonishment and decided to tell me more about the trip.

She was in a cafe one day and saw a motor bike hit a pedestrian. She jumped up and yelled at the driver to stop. He drove off without even slowing down. The cafe people pulled the victim to the side of the road as if this type of incident happened routinely and called his family. His legs appeared to be broken. No one called an ambulance or took him to the hospital. The family collected him not long after.

When she questioned the cafe staff about it, they said the victim would receive $500 as compensation. If he had died, the family would receive $1,000. Cam concluded, "I clearly understood how much the government thinks a life is worth."

My mouth must have fallen open, because Cam paused and gave me a hard look, as if she were telling a naive teenager about the dangers of walking alone at night.

"On that trip, I learned that the president of Vietnam and his family had fled to Paris before the South Vietnamese army was defeated. He later sneaked into the US and was recognized and chased. The US government wanted to prosecute him, but didn't catch him. I'm sorry they didn't."

I said nothing.

Cam delivered her final missive in a bitter voice. "My uncle told me that right before the fall of the South Vietnamese army, the top general invited all his officers to his home for a sumptuous dinner. Right after the meal, the general excused himself and went upstairs where he shot himself in the head. He did not want to be caught."

Without looking at me, she excused herself to find her children. It took me a few minutes to recover. This was a side of Cam I had never seen before.

*****

I headed for the table where William and Vi Nguyen, the handsome couple who lived part time in Saigon and part time in California, were eating a fruit dessert. She wore a beautiful peach suit with pearl earrings and a stunning necklace of pearls and lapis. William was handsome in a perfectly tailored cream colored suit and subtle gray tie.

I was hoping for a change of pace from Cam's disturbing diatribe. Maybe we could have a more genial conversation.

They greeted me cordially, recalling I was Cam's English teacher. William stood and pulled out a chair for me. Vi asked in her formal British English, "Have you enjoyed meeting our family, Miss O'Neil?"

"I've loved it, and please call me Callie." I was still quaking inside from Cam's bitterness.

"Delighted," Vi responded.

"May I ask you a question, if you don't mind? I'm struggling with understanding the different experiences native Vietnamese immigrants living in the US have had compared to their children who were born and raised here."

William nodded, and Vi answered, "Of course. What would you want to know?"

I chose my words carefully, not wanting to offend. "What were the greatest challenges your relatives faced when they settled in the US or Canada?"

William asked, "Do you mean boat people or later immigrants?"

"Boat people," I answered but actually was curious about both.

"Language." William and Vi said the word together and smiled at each other the way couples do when they've been together for decades. I felt a stab of envy.

William continued. "Some left professional jobs in Vietnam. They were wealthy and respected in their communities. Others were not so fortunate. Their lives were simple. But most Vietnamese in the 1960s and 1970s did not speak English. The ones that spoke French were no better off when they came here."

Vi picked up her husband's train of thought. "Vietnamese immigrants to America shared the challenge of both learning a new language and earning a living. Language skills were essential for supporting their families. And most Vietnamese arrived without language and without money."

"How did they survive?" I asked.

William answered, "Any way they could. Professors became janitors. Their wives cleaned houses or worked in beauty parlors or restaurants. Church sponsors deserve our everlasting gratitude for finding them jobs and caring for their children while they attended English classes at night."

Vi continued, "Vietnamese communities grew up wherever churches had sponsored refugees, and the communities eventually took over the roles of the sponsors. Families cared for each other's children, repaired each other's homes, and became extended families."

I considered this evolution for a moment. "What do you think their children's greatest challenges are – the refugees' children?"

William and Vi exchanged a look. William cleared his throat and answered carefully. "I think the answer to your question depends greatly on how closely the Vietnamese parents, the immigrants, adhered to their Vietnamese culture."

"I'm not sure I understand. Can you explain?" I asked.

Vi nodded, "William is correct. If the parents remained religious, Buddhist or Christian, and instilled traditional Vietnamese values of respect and hard work, the children would grow up much the way they would have in Vietnam. But if both parents worked, the children would be on their own and would probably become far more Americanized quickly, both in language and culture." I couldn't tell if they thought this was a good or bad thing, but surmised that preserving their Vietnamese culture was preferable.

I would ask Tony about this the next time I had a chance.

I was very curious about this attractive couple and cautiously asked, "If you don't mind my asking, do you live in two countries because of your business or is this your choice?"

William answered readily. "Both actually. I'm in the import/export business. We have offices in Ho Chi Minh City and in Los Angeles." I noted that William was the first person not to call the capital Saigon.

"Would you mind telling me a little about your background, William? You and Vi seem somehow different from others I've met here. For one thing, you're the only ones still living in Vietnam."

William considered for a moment, then said, "I'd be happy to share some of my story with you, Callie. But if you don't mind, I'll start after I settled in California. I'm sure you've heard tales about escaping from Vietnam, so I won't bore you with mine."

Of course, that made his escape story more intriguing, but I understood he didn't intend to share it. "Of course, William, wherever you care to start is fine with me."

"I attended Cal Poly College. The U.S. government helped by paying my health insurance. I worked part time at JC Penny's as a stock boy to support myself. I volunteered to stay late and gift wrap difficult purchases, such as an entertainment center a man was giving his family. After a few months, I was assigned as stock boy to the shoe department where the sales staff worked on commission."

Vi reached for William's hand and interwove her fingers with his. This story obviously touched her as well.

William continued, "The department manager liked the way I volunteered to work after closing hours to finish up whatever needed doing. Eventually, I worked my way up to a sales position. I figured out that our customers who worked in Silicon Valley needed anti-static shoes. So I drove to a chip factory with a Penny's catalogue and took orders for anti-static shoes. The customers were happy they didn't have to shop in person."

William looked directly at me and said matter-of-factly, "I delivered shoes in my old Ford, and my commissions grew to $50,000 a year, far more than other sales people. So much more that the manager suspected that I'd convinced other sales staff to use my employee number when ringing up their sales."

I interrupted, "You would never do that!" What an idiot I was. I had just met this man.

William smiled, "No, I wouldn't. HR assigned someone to spy on me (peeking through the lingerie department) and discovered that the sales were legitimately mine."

He paused and exchanged a fond look with Vi.

"I graduated with a business major and accepted a job as plant supervisor for a textile manufacturer in Los Angeles. One thing led to another. Now I have my own company with offices in Hanoi, Ho Chi Minh City, and Los Angeles. My goal is to increase trade between the US and Vietnam, regardless of politics."

That seemed to be all William intended to say, so I asked Vi, "How did you and William meet?"

She smiled graciously, still holding her husband's hand. "My family are British, as you can surmise. I worked with my father in the tea business. William and I met at a trade conference in Washington D.C. For me, it was what Americans call love at first sight." I saw William squeeze her fingers.

I sensed I had intruded enough with my questions and thanked them for their thoughtfulness in sharing their stories with me. As I turned to leave, I made a mental note to ask Tony about a comment he had made recently about American companies doing business with Vietnam.

I was half way across the room, when I felt a tap on my shoulder. I turned to see Vi, her eyes sparkling.

"Callie, have you met Chi? He lives in Kauai."

"No, Vi, I haven't."

"After your questions to us, William and I thought you'd find his story interesting on its own and quite different from others you've heard in the past few days."

"I'd love to meet him."

"Then follow me and I'll introduce you. He's right over there." Vi pointed to a knot of men talking quietly near the buffet table.

Vi graciously interrupted them. "Excuse me, cousins. Chi, I'd like to introduce you to Cam's English teacher, Callie. If you have a few minutes, she'd like to talk to you."

I shook hands with an extremely fit, middle aged man, who beamed at me. His hand shake was firm, his hands calloused but immaculate. His shaved head reminded me of Yul Brynner, as did his penetrating dark eyes. A very handsome man, simply dressed in jeans and a glowing white tee shirt that showed off bulging biceps.

Chi excused himself from his cousins. "How can I help, Callie?" His accent combined Vietnamese and Pacific Island pidgin.

"I'm fascinated by your family's stories, Chi. And Vi suggested I ask you about how you came to the US. Do you mind sharing it with me?"

"Of course not. Let's walk while we talk. Is that OKAY? I've been to the buffet many too many times in the last few days."

"I'd like that." We headed to Old Town.

Chapter 26
Chi's Story

The French were waging war in Indonesia during the 1950s. We lived in a poor village outside Saigon. My father was a chef in the French navy and gone most of the time. Eventually, he stopped coming home. My mother tried her best. She worked in her family's restaurant where lots of Frenchmen came to eat and to drink.

We were beyond poor, as was much of our village. We shared an outdoor toilet with the rest of the village. My grandmother was a "stay-at-home" mom and raised me and my two brothers. My grandfather was the tallest man in the village. He was a singer with a traveling circus.

Mom earned a meager living from her take of the drinks she enticed the French clients to order. Her dream was for one of the Frenchmen to marry her and take her family to Paris. She never asked if they were married.

She became pregnant with my brother, Etienne, by one of these Frenchmen. He didn't take her to Paris. She was equally unsuccessful with my brother Louis's father. He didn't take her to Paris, either. My French father

195

didn't want us, either. Three definitely was not the charm for my mom. I never met my father.

My brothers and I slept together in a wooden bed. When we had fallen asleep, my grandmother socialized with her friends, playing cards and gossiping. My mom was at work. One of my first memories was waking up and crying when I couldn't find my grandmother. I knew that my mother wouldn't be home for hours.

The French living in Vietnam were avid Catholics, which didn't seem to impact the men's sexual activities. The Church tried to reunite the bastard Vietnamese/French children with their fathers who had returned to France.

My mother sent Etienne to France with the nuns, hoping he would have a better life there. He was nine. Etienne was not reunited with his father. He finished school when he was 17, ran around Paris, joined the French army, served his time, lived under a bridge back in Paris. He eventually met his wife and learned to be a medical technician. He lives a happy life in Paris. Mom was right.

Louis was a rascal right from birth. My mom knew he wouldn't behave if she sent him to the nuns in France. Instead, he was sent to a Catholic orphanage in Tours. He was not allowed to speak Vietnamese at the orphanage and was out of control with frustration from not knowing the language. He hit a nun with a broom one day after being punished for not obeying an order he didn't understand.

Louis eventually learned to read and write English, but his spoken skills were poor. He and mom exchanged letters in Vietnamese.

My mom finally met a Danish man who agreed to take care of her and me. He already had a daughter with a Danish woman. Mom didn't tell him about her other two sons. Johan adopted me and moved us to Washington DC, because he thought that would be a safe place for us to live. He was in the merchant marines and traveled a lot.

In 1968, the US Navy needed Johan to help them navigate the Mekong River so they could deliver supplies. His life was in grave danger, since the Viet Cong and the Americans were constantly trying to blow each other up.

After they had been married several years, my mother told Johan about her other two sons. When my grandmother died in Vietnam, Johan managed to locate Louis in France and sent him to Saigon to take care of my grandparents. Johan provided the three of them with a house and money.

My grandmother died five years later. Louis lost the house and spent all of the money. By this time, South Vietnam had fallen to the North. Half breeds like Louis were being rounded up by the victors. Louis hid in a Buddhist temple, but the army found him and dragged him into the jungle to work on rubber trees. He escaped in the late 1970s and lived in hiding with friends in Saigon.

I was 13 in 1968 when Johan took us to Washington DC. I cried when I said good-bye to my grandparents outside the airport. We flew on Pan Am to Hanoi, then to Guam, and finally to Seattle. I didn't speak a word of English. Neither did my mother.

I was supposed to be in seventh grade, but the school put me back two grades. I had left school in Vietnam because we didn't have money to pay tuition. School isn't free there like it is in the U.S.

Math was the only subject I understood. Everything else sounded like blah, blah, blah. I was in lots of fights. The other kids called me nip or Jap and told me to go home. My mother asked why I was always in trouble.

One teacher took pity on me and offered to tutor me in English in her home.

After school, I took care of our small house because Johan was away at sea. I walked to school, which was nearby. But in high school, I walked four miles each way in the biting cold and wind because we didn't have the money for bus fare. I learned to take short cuts through people's property. I ran fast and hid when I heard someone coming.

There were no Vietnamese kids in high school until my junior year. Sam was a boat person and we became friends. Our white neighbors weren't used to foreigners and were hostile to us, so I didn't make friends with the kids who lived nearby. Instead, I got involved in sports.

When my step-dad came home, he was furious at me for my bad grades. He accused me of not trying. He didn't understand that my poor English was why I failed. Mom was caught in the middle. It was very tense when Johan was home. No one was happy.

I made a friend on the track team. The coach paired Jacob and me to race during practice. Jacob was proud he was the fastest kid on the team. But I beat him and we became friends.

He invited me to his house. His dad worked for the electric company, and his mom was a beautician. If Jacob didn't get good grades, his dad didn't get mad at him and accuse him of not trying.

After several months, Jacob's family invited me to live in their basement, where Ann, the mom, had her salon. I did chores for her in exchange for room and board. She made sure I did my homework and was the single biggest reason I graduated from high school.

Ann also fought the school district when they tried to implement segregation. They wanted me to be bused miles away from the house. Ann won.

My mom felt guilty that I had to live with another family. But she had seen me struggle with Johan for two years and knew I would be happier with Jacob's family. I think she still feels guilty, which makes me sad. She did her best, and I always knew she loved me. She did what she had to do.

I quit sports after I moved to Jacob's house so I could take a part time job and pay Ann something. I gave her $35 a week, just to help out.

I became a US citizen in 1976.

After graduation, I spent $600, most of my savings, on a Chevy Nova and drove to California by myself. I had no idea if the car would make it. I talked to a lot of strangers in coffee shops and gas stations. I was broke when I arrived in Orange County, south of Los Angeles.

I couldn't find a job, so I joined the Navy and was sent to San Diego. They put me through training, but I didn't pass the test. So they put me through training again. I failed the test again. The officers knew I wasn't stupid and didn't understand why I couldn't pass the test. They had watched me lead our platoon in marching exercises and knew I was capable. So they put me in a special program. I answered the questions in class, but failed the written test for the third time.

I told the officer the Navy was wasting their time with me. Neither he nor I recognized that I didn't have the skills to take written tests, even though I had mastered the material. The Navy granted me an honorable discharge.

The old Chevy and I headed back to Seattle. Ann suggested I investigate Job Corps, which turned out to be a great idea. I completed an eight-week carpentry course and joined a union. I rode my bike from my single room in North Seattle to the city center. I didn't understand the bus system, so I got up at 4:30 a.m. and arrived at 7:00 for work.

A kindly Japanese couple rented me a room in their basement for $300 a month.

The union sent me to So. Seattle to work on low income housing renovations as an apprentice. I did well and was given more responsible assignments. But it was too cold in Seattle, and I was unhappy.

I went to the library and studied a map of the U.S. I saw the beautiful blue ocean and a sprinkle of islands in the Pacific. Hawaii. When I went to a travel agency, the woman suggested I go to Kauai. So I bought a ticket. The night before the flight, I was visiting a friend and didn't realize that my wallet had fallen behind between the sofa seats.

In those days, you just had to show your ticket to board a plane. I didn't have any ID or money. A year later, my friend found my wallet and mailed it to my mom.

No one in my family knew where I was. I had only a pack back when I arrived in Lihue. I hitchhiked to Princeville. When I look back on that time, I understand that I had lost all hope. I thought it was my time to die. I had nothing and no one. Someone told me about a trail into the jungle that led to nowhere. I hiked in and lived in the jungle. I had nothing to lose.

I don't know where I got the strength to hike out of the jungle. I hitchhiked to Lihue and went to the police station. I met Tanaka, the officer in charge, and told him I was hungry and homeless. He let me sleep in a cell. He sent someone to get food and made some phone calls.

A couple in Kapa'a offered to let me stay with them. Tanaka drove me in a police car to their small church and parsonage. The couple were from North Carolina. He had just been ordained and explained he needed help taking care of the church.

My job was to open the church on Sundays before service and clean up afterward. I found another job at a construction company, digging ditches for $5 an hour. I was 22 when I met an older Japanese couple at church who invited me to live in a shack on their property, right on the beach.

I met my first wife when I was 26 and married her when I was 30, after graduating from community college.

I'm 62 years old and feel healthier and happier than I have in my entire life. My custom carpentry business is booming. I'm a grandfather. I'm still shy about my English, but my customers are kind and willing to fill in the words I don't know or mispronounce. My mom lives nearby in Kauai. Her husband had a stroke and lives in a care facility down the road.

I visited Vietnam in 2001, 2002 and 2005. The first visit was scary. I was afraid because of my American passport. Ex-Vietnamese were not welcome. Things have gotten much better.

I'm a lucky man.

Chapter 27

Dan

Time was running out. The reunion would be over in just a few hours. I realized the only way to find an answer to the question of what challenges the new generation of Vietnamese-Americans experience was to ask the cousins directly. I looked for Sherry and found Cam instead, followed by her children wrapped in towels, still dripping from the pool.

"Hi Callie, you're looking thoughtful. Is there something I can help you with?" She seemed to have recovered from her angry outburst and had reverted to the charming woman I was used to.

"Hi Cam. Yes, you can. Have you seen Sherry?"

"She's outside with her cousins. I saw them by the pool. But I need to warn you – it's scorching outside."

"Thanks for the warning. I'll see you later." I turned away, knowing I could catch up with Cam later.

Cam was right. The sun was punishing outside.

Sherry and the same four cousins I'd met before were sitting in the Jacuzzi apparently unfazed by the heat. Sherry's brother, Dan was with them. I wasn't sure how to approach the group and wished I'd had my bathing suit so I could join them casually. Instead, Sherry glanced over at me and immediately left the pool to greet me.

"Hi, Miss O'Neil. Can you join us?"

Without thinking I answered, "Sure, if no one objects to a nude 40-year old." The cousins were shocked, then burst out laughing. Dan shouted, "Come as you are. We don't mind." Which caused more laughter.

Sherry looked conflicted, wanting to laugh at the same time as showing respect. I touched her wet shoulder. "It's Okay, Sherry, I asked for it."

She grinned. "Is there something I can help you with?"

"As a matter of fact, you and your cousins can help me. When you're finished with the Jacuzzi, could we spend a few minutes together, all of you?"

"Sure." Sherry sounded uncertain and returned to the group. In less than a minute, I was surrounded by six dripping young people. They smelled of sun block. I ushered them to a table with an umbrella away from the pool. "Dan, I'm happy to meet you." He shook my outstretched hand with his wet one. I noticed he had several tattoos scattered on his back, his neck, one leg and both arms.

Dan looked friendly. "You, too. Sherry told me about you. She said you were cool." I mouthed "thank you" to Sherry.

I addressed the group, "May I ask you a few questions?" They glanced sideways at each other, and I sensed their apprehension. "I'm not the police or FBI, I'm just curious about some of the conversations I've had in the past couple of days and would like your opinions."

Sherry chirped, "Okay, fire away." She was beautiful in a miniscule black bikini.

They placed their towels on their chairs, sat down and looked at me attentively. I felt I was back in the classroom, but with very well behaved students. I began as casually as I could. "Do any of you speak Vietnamese?"

Robert answered, "No, I don't, but I understand most of what my parents say to each other." Kate nodded in agreement.

Dan sneered, "Not only no, but hell no! I have no interest in speaking Vietnamese." Everyone was quiet, Sherry looked down in embarrassment.

"Dan, why do you feel so strongly?" I asked.

His reply was angry. "Because the sooner immigrants become Americans, the better off we'll all be." He paused, then continued more rationally. "Speaking Vietnamese keeps my parents from acclimating to the US. It separates them, which seems to be what they want. If they had the chance, I'm sure they'd return to Vietnam, but not under the communists. The US will never be their home."

"Do you agree?" I asked the others.

Kate, a moon-faced young woman with intelligent eyes, offered, "Dan's point is valid. But it doesn't take into account the comfort my parents feel speaking their own language in what is still a foreign country. I was encouraged to speak only English when I was a child. My parents didn't want me to experience the mortification they felt when they arrived here from the camp."

I asked her, "Do you wish you could speak Vietnamese?"

Without hesitation, Kate responded, "Absolutely. I understand what Robert was saying, but I want to visit Vietnam and speak to the people there. I would love to be bi-lingual."

I turned to Dan, "Do you ever feel like that?"

His face was shut tight. "No, I don't. Vietnam means nothing to me."

"How about you, Andrew?" I asked.

He was an extremely handsome young man, well built with classic features and perfectly groomed hair. "I have to admit, I'm ambivalent. My parents are traditional, which means they expect me to get top grades and show them respect by doing what they want me to. I owe them so much, knowing what they've sacrificed for me and my sister." He paused.

"But what, Andrew?" I wanted him to complete his thought.

"Well, for example, my girlfriend is Mexican-American. My parents are not pleased. We'll leave it at that. They don't understand why I don't have a Vietnamese girlfriend. And they want me to be a doctor, just like all their parents." He gestured to the group. "But I have no interest in medicine. I'm not sure what I want to do, but I know it will be something in marketing. My parents don't understand what marketing even is."

Dan chimed in, "See what I mean?"

Sherry added, "Miss O'Neil, we're children of immigrants. We appreciate and love our parents. We all talk about being grateful to them for giving up their lives in Vietnam, but at the same time, we feel we're Americans or Canadians. It can be very difficult for us."

Dan interrupted his sister, "It's not difficult for me. I just do as I please. They can like it or not, but I'm not living their lives and they're not living mine."

This was met with silence. Then Wayne spoke for the first time. He was a slight, pale teenager, shy and quiet. He said softly, looking at Dan, "Man, I hear you, but I don't feel angry like you do. I feel sad for what my parents lost. And I feel hopeful that I'll choose my own career, whatever that is. I just don't want to give up my family by fighting all the time." He looked away.

Sherry reached across the table and placed her hand on Wayne's shoulder. "You are one of the smartest kids in our school. You're going to be amazing at whatever you do. Your parents will be proud of you."

Dan snickered, "Good dog, Wayne."

207

Sherry's eyes flashed at her brother, "That's inappropriate, Dan. You owe Wayne an apology. We're not all like you. I respect your dreams, but I don't have to follow the path you take to realize them."

Dan looked abashed and muttered. "Okay, okay. Sorry, Wayne." Sherry's opinion obviously meant something to him.

Sherry turned back to Wayne and said with great compassion, "I'm sorry you had such a miserable time, Wayne. It shouldn't be that way, especially in California."

He responded, "I've had a crush on this girl in my bio class. We've done a few projects together, so it's not like I don't know her. When I finally got up the nerve to ask her to the prom, she looked at me like I had a disease. She said she didn't date Asian guys and walked away. I was mortified."

Sherry reached for his hand, "Wayne, she doesn't deserve you. When you're a neural surgeon and she brings her kid to you for surgery, I wonder if she'll remember how she treated you." Wayne simply shrugged.

There was an uncomfortable silence. I broke it by asking, "I've been told that your parents' greatest challenge when they came to America was learning the language. Would you agree?"

Sherry was the first to answer. "Yes. My mom said the church sponsors were really kind to them, but they couldn't converse. The church ladies stocked our apartment with loads of canned food – stuff like tuna, which my parents found disgusting."

Robert joined in. "My mom said it took her six months of English classes before she could explain to the church ladies that our family ate rice."

Everyone laughed. He went on. "My parents packed up all the canned stuff and returned it to the church. Two church members finally drove to Chicago and bought a 50-pound sack of rice. My mom made a deal with the butcher to buy chicken necks which she cooked with the rice. She said she had been hungry for the first six months in Wisconsin."

Sherry commented, "Miss O'Neil, I think all of my generation would agree that our parents' biggest challenge was language. But finding work was just as important. Vietnamese people are proud. They don't want to ask for anything."

Kate added, "My dad tells everyone that he found a job two weeks after coming to the US and was never on welfare."

Robert said, "Same with my dad. He was a successful businessman in Saigon. He hated taking money from the church sponsors. The third month after he immigrated, he and my mom started paying our apartment rent. He's really proud of that."

Dan didn't comment. His silence was loud.

I went on, "Then what would you say your greatest challenges are as first generation Americans or Canadians?"

They exchanged thoughtful looks. Sherry was the first to speak. "I think balancing my parents' culture with my own American identity. I want to be respectful, but I also need to be independent and make my own choices."

Kate said, "Me, too. I agree with Sherry."

I was surprised when Wayne spoke up. "Making friends." We all gaped at him, waiting for more. He glanced around, then softly explained. "There were no Asian kids in my first school. Only one black kid. No one would talk to me. I ate lunch by myself. I was really lonely."

I asked gently, "How about now, Wayne?"

"I'm in the gifted program, so I've made friends with several kids in the program. But if you asked what was my biggest problem being an immigrant, it was being lonely. I looked different. I spoke some English, but I was an outsider and so were my family."

Robert nodded. "It got better as I got older. When we moved to California from Indiana, there were a lot more Asian kids in my classes. I have both Asian and non-Asian friends now, and it doesn't seem to matter."

Kate agreed. "California is really the best state for Vietnamese. I want to go to Berkeley for college. There are a ton of Asians there."

Sherry sighed, then asked me what time it was. I was the only one with a watch. "It's five-thirty." The group all jumped up, except for Dan. "We have to get ready for dinner," Sherry explained as they grabbed their towels and rushed into the hotel. Dan gave me a measured look, then turned away and went back into the Jacuzzi.

"Bye, Dan. See you later."

"Miss O'Neil!" Dan motioned me over. With fierce concentration he looked me right in the eye, "I need to be emancipated. Just like the American slaves."

"I'm sure you'll succeed, Dan."

He closed his eyes dismissing me as he sunk back into the hot water.

*****

Everyone dressed for the final reunion dinner. Many of the women wore gorgeous Vietnamese silks. I had bought a new sundress – white with navy trim. It looked cool and tidy, I thought as I coiled my hair to beat the heat.

Thu and Tony picked me up, right on time as always.

"Thu, I haven't had a chance to talk to you in two days! Where have you been?" I asked her.

She smiled, "I've been here. It's you who has been busy. I've watched you go from elder to younger, then in between."

I laughed, thinking she was right. I'd tried to make the most of my time at the reunion. "I guess I've been doing a lot of talking and listening. It's been a wonderful experience." Tony and Thu looked happy with my response.

Thu narrowed her eyes at me and asked, "Tran has been speaking to us in Vietnamese. Is it because he's at a family reunion or did you suggest this?"

I evaded her question. "Maybe both, Thu. Are you Okay if he uses both languages?"

"I am very happy he wants to practice Vietnamese." Phew! I changed the subject.

"Tony, what time are you leaving tomorrow?"

He hesitated. "We've had a slight change in plans. We're staying one more day. I have some business to attend to. We'll leave very early the next day." He didn't explain his business, and I didn't ask, although I wanted to.

"I guess I won't see you then."

"Not 'til we're home." I felt a little hollow pit in my stomach, or was it my heart?

Thu said, "Callie, will you come for dinner when we get home? Tran is very anxious for you to talk to the PE teacher about pickleball. And Tony and I want to hear about your conversations with the family."

"I would love to, thanks, Thu. I'll wait until you've unpacked and done the laundry." Thu laughed.

As I lay in bed that night, I thought about Thu. How had I spent three very busy days with her extended family and had hardly seen her? She had obviously observed me talking and listening to old and young Vong family members.

I remembered the first time I'd seen her in Tom's office. Quiet, shy, letting Tony and Tran do the talking. I reflected on the other occasions we'd both attended. She walked into a room without causing any attention. She observed what was happening, but the air and space around her remained still. Yet, when I had questions about Tony or Tran, it was Thu I wanted to consult.

My last waking thought was that Thu could teach me some valuable lessons.

Chapter 28

Home

Thu's invitation to dinner was on my phone the following weekend. I had been catching up with my writing class essays but was really looking forward to seeing Tran, Thu and Tony. I'd been dying to talk to Cam, too, but she and her family were still in California, taking the children to Disneyland and Universal Studios.

I arrived at the appointed time with a tin of chocolate chip cookies I'd baked that morning. Tran immediately accepted the tin, opened it and stuffed a cookie into his mouth. Thu looked shocked at his boldness, but Tony laughed. "I guess you chose the right dinner contribution." Tran looked sheepish, then thanked me politely for the cookies. I realized I'd never heard Thu correct Tran.

We spent the evening discussing their drive home, how I'd been spending my time, and finally worked around to Thu's question about how I liked the reunion.

"I don't know how to explain it, Thu. I felt honored to be invited, and so fortunate to share your family's heroic stories."

She asked, "What do you mean, Callie?"

I tried again, "My family were Irish farmers who left their country during the potato famine. Their families were starving, and there were no jobs for them off the farm. I'm not saying they weren't suffering.

They boarded ships, sailed across the Atlantic Ocean, glimpsed the Statue of Liberty and stopped at Ellis Island. They settled in Irish neighborhoods in New York or Boston. They looked like the people around them. They spoke English, although with accents. They became policemen, painters, carpenters, bar tenders, waiters, and so on."

Thu still looked confused. "How is our family different? We are also refugees."

"That's right, Thu," I agreed. "There are certainly similarities. But there are huge differences, too. Your relatives were abused by the communists. Your family risked their lives escaping in fishing boats. They saw their friends and family members die of starvation on the way. They spent months, even years, in camps, not knowing if they would ever find sponsors."

"That is true." Thu agreed.

"And they didn't speak English," I continued. "When they finally settled here, the children went to schools where they were the only Asians." I was getting worked up, and I heard my voice rising.

Tony interrupted and placed his hand on my shoulder. "Callie, it was wonderful having you at the reunion. And excellent that you met our family. But we look to the future, not the past. Our reunion was a celebration of survival."

"Please forgive me. I was out of line to focus on the negative parts of your lives." I felt like a cat in the rain.

Tran looked directly at me. "Miss O'Neil, we Vietnamese make wonderful Americans."

I wanted to cry, but laughed instead. "Tran, you certainly do. I think I need a hug." Tran walked over to me and shyly gave me the briefest hug, then stepped back.

"Tran, do you think you could call me Callie when we're not in school."

He considered my question and answered gravely, "No, I don't think so."

I hooted and raised my palm for a high five which he readily gave me. "Okay, I'll always be Miss O'Neil. That'll work." Thu and Tony were smiling.

Tony cleared his throat, a sure sign he had something important to say. "Callie, I want to tell you about my extra day in California."

"Good, I didn't want to ask you, but I'm very curious."

"You are always curious. It's one of your best character traits. In fact, it's contagious." He grinned at me. "Now I'll tell you what I did. I interviewed at Golden Gate University Law School."

I was speechless, something that rarely happened. "Tell me more, Tony," I managed.

He looked at his sister and politely asked, "Thu, do you mind if Callie and I take a walk?"

She nodded her agreement. Tony ushered - me out the door, and we headed down the street, strolling by sleepy houses. I waited for Tony to begin.

"Not long ago you asked me about my dreams."

"I remember, in Pasadena. I'm anxious to hear about them."

"I've wanted to go to law school for a long time. It has been my dream since living in America, but life had more important things for me to do first."

"Like escaping, learning English, earning a living, caring for your sister and your cousin."

"Exactly. But now I'm in a position to return to my dreams. I've taken and passed the LSAT. That's why I needed your help with writing."

I stopped walking and turned to him in astonishment. "Why didn't you tell me, Tony?"

He looked uncomfortable and murmured, "Because I didn't want you to know if I failed."

I took his hand and squeezed it. I didn't know what to say. He squeezed back. "The good news is that I've been accepted at Golden Gate and will start law school in September."

"Does that mean you'll be moving to Los Angeles?" I felt a lump of ice form in my throat.

"Yes."

"With Thu and Tran?" My voice was wary.

"Of course."

We had stopped walking. Tony faced me and placed his hands on my shoulders. "Callie, we would like you to come with us."

I stared at him in disbelief. "What did you say, Tony?"

"I think you heard me, Callie. I asked you to come with us."

I was still in shock, "In September, in six weeks, quit my job, both jobs, sell my condo, and move to LA while you go to law school. Is that correct?"

I felt him trying to stifle a laugh. "Correct. Remember, Callie, we Vietnamese are survivors."

I wasn't laughing. "But I'm not Vietnamese, Tony. I have a contract with the school. I have a mortgage and car payments. I don't have a job in LA."

He answered glibly, "But you look like everyone else in LA and you speak excellent English. It will be easy for you, like an Irishwoman." Now I had to laugh with him.

"That's true, Tony. Maybe I could learn to speak Spanish."

He grinned. "Speaking of speaking Spanish, I've done a little research for you."

I was amazed at this conversation. "What kind of research?"

"The placement office at Golden Gate gave me some information about ESL teaching positions. There are several openings in LA, some for teaching adults and some for teaching Spanish-speaking kids. I have a folder for you with all the job postings."

When I didn't respond, Tony added, "I found out that you will need to get a California teaching credential to teach in the public schools, but there are several private schools looking for qualified instructors."

I didn't know what to say. After a pause I asked him, "I suppose you've also looked at housing options."

He grinned. "That's right. Your Pasadena friends have offered their guest house until you find a place of your own. Or ..." he stopped speaking.

"Or what, Tony?"

His voice was strained and anxious. He didn't look at me when he answered. "We could rent a house that's big enough for the four of us."

I spent a minute calculating my response. "Tony, I don't know what to say. I hadn't expected we'd be having this conversation, and I'm not even sure what you are proposing."

He bent toward me slowly and gently kissed my lips, just for a moment. "Callie, I'm not sure either. I just know how I feel about you. I don't want to live so far from you before we give ourselves a chance."

"I see." It was all I could say, but the familiar flutter was back in my stomach, and I wished the kiss had been longer.

"Please think about it and we'll talk more when you're ready." He turned around and waited for me to follow him back to his home.

I tugged his sleeve to keep him from walking. "Have you discussed this with Thu? And with Tran?"

"Of course. Thu is hoping you will accept. She feels you are her sister. I have not talked to Tran. He would be very disappointed if you refused. He has suffered enough losses in his short life. I don't want to add any more."

That was the last of our conversation that evening. Needless to say, I didn't get much sleep that night. I wondered if Tony had.

Chapter 29

Lien's Story

Advanced ESL writing class resumed the first week of August. I was excited to see Cam again and hoped we'd have time to talk before or after class.

Lien placed a fresh sheet on top of the others. Shyly she said she'd written several chapters of her memoir, but didn't want to overburden me the first day of class. "I'll give them to you one at a time. Or would you rather have them all together?"

"One at a time will be perfect," I responded. "That way I can spend time with each episode."

Unfortunately, Cam was distracted that evening. Her daughter had a bad cold, so she rushed away as soon as class was over, but she promised to submit an essay the following week.

I couldn't sleep that night either. Rather than toss and turn, I decided to read Lien's story.

My husband Van's first wife was in the military where they met. She became a businesswoman when she left the Army. Her business of "helping" people escape from Vietnam earned her 14 years in jail.

Here's how she cheated people. She charged ten ounces of gold to help them leave Vietnam, with a two-ounce down payment. She collected the down payment and told her clients she'd call them when the actual escape date had been fixed.

Not long after the first meeting, she contacted her clients to return their down payments because the authorities had become aware of the plan. The clients immediately trusted her for refunding their gold.

In a few days she called them again and told them to bring the entire payment, since a departure date had been set. They met in a church where she collected all the gold. While she was explaining how they should pack for the trip, the authorities raided the church and confiscated all the gold. The people fled back to their homes. Van's wife split the gold with her friends, the authorities.

I was appalled at this story, but knew it must have been true. I wrote an A on Lien's paper.

After another restless night of flailing then waking, I experienced an overpowering need to confide in someone. Not my mother or my sister with whom I simply didn't share my feelings. Who then? The answer came like a bolt – Thu. I called her that morning. "Thu, will you have lunch with me today? I really need to talk to you."

"Yes, of course. I was expecting your call." Her English was improving, and she was obviously aware of the situation. We agreed to meet at noon.

She was waiting in a booth at the back of the coffee shop where it was quiet. I wasn't late, but she had already ordered iced coffee.

"Thank you for meeting me, Thu. I'm so confused and just needed to talk to you."

She inclined her head and waited for me to speak. "Tony told me his plans for moving to LA and going to law school."

She responded, "That has been his dream for many years."

I asked, "Did he want to be a lawyer when he was growing up in Vietnam?"

"I don't think so. He started his dream when we came to this country."

"Why?" I asked bluntly.

"You need to ask Tony. He will tell you."

"Okay, I'll do that. Now for the big question, at least the big one for me. He wants me to come with you. I still can't believe it." I said this more to myself than to Thu.

"Tony wants us to be a family."

I was stunned. "A family?" I asked stupidly.

"Tony and I did not have children. This makes us very sad. The war came and ruined our chances." Thu looked stricken for a moment, then brightened. "But God sent us Tran. He is like a son to us."

"Thu, did you ever love someone you wanted to marry?"

She looked directly at me as she answered. "Yes, a student in my class. He was from Hanoi. He was forced to join the communist army during the war. He was killed by American forces."

I automatically reached for her hand. "Oh Thu, I'm so sorry. And here you are living in America. Are you bitter?"

"What is bitter?" she asked.

"Sort of angry that your lover was killed by people from the country where you now live."

"No bitter. Sad and sometimes lonely."

I realized she and I shared many of the same feelings. But my husband hadn't been killed. He just drifted away. However, I imagined we shared the same sense of loss, unfulfillment and longing.

"Have you met anyone else since you've lived here?"

"No."

I knew I shouldn't ask Thu about Tony's past. She was too respectful of her brother to discuss his personal issues. So I focused on their plans.

"How do you feel about moving to LA?"

"Good. We have family in California. Weather is more like Vietnam." Then she lowered her gaze and her voice. "I have my own plan for LA."

"Can you tell me?"

"Yes," she smiled. "You are like my sister." I smiled back and waited.

"I will go to secretarial school in LA. I studied in Vietnam, but never worked in America. I can work and help Tony with expenses."

Without thinking, I said, "Thu, I can help you get ready for school, if you'd like. I don't start teaching middle school for another month. We could study together."

She beamed at me and took my hand. "I am grateful. I know my English is bad, but I am a hard-working Vietnamese."

I squeezed her hand. "I know you are. And you are so kind." I continued, "How do you think Tran will feel about moving?"

She was thoughtful. "Tran is a good boy. He will do what we ask him."

I tried again. "But will he want to leave?"

"I don't know. He doesn't say."

I guessed that Tran wouldn't want to leave Hanna Lund, now that they were friends. "Do you mind if I ask him?"

"Please talk to Tran. He likes you. He may tell you what is in his heart."

"I'll do that, Thu." The waitress came to take our order. When she left, I approached the subject I really wanted to discuss.

"Thu, Tony suggested we rent a house where we all could live. How do you feel about that?"

Her smile transformed her plain face into a lovely one. "In Vietnamese culture, families live together. When a son marries, he brings his wife to live with his parents. Tony and I can't follow this, but we can make a family of our own with you and Tran."

Speechless again. And that wondrous feeling that I was way out of my league. There was a part of me longing for this type of commitment, but another part that screamed "Are you crazy? Giving up your job and your privacy to join a Vietnamese family? You hardly know them!"

Thu must have read the conflict on my face. She patted my hand. "No need to decide today."

Our food arrived, and I think we both appreciated the distraction.

Chapter 30

Law School

Tony called me that night and asked me to have dinner with him the next night, which conflicted with my class. But I suggested the following evening. When we hung up, I realized we had never been on a formal date, and here he was asking me to live with him. Well sort of. Asking me to live with his family was more accurate.

I dressed with care on date night. I wanted to look attractive, but not seductive. When I passed over my red dress, I had another of those mirror conversations with myself. "What's wrong with the red dress? Well, it's sexy. What's wrong with sexy? It will give Tony the wrong idea. You want to make love with him, right? Right. But you're afraid to show him? Maybe. What are you afraid of? Be honest now. Pause. I don't want another failure – is that honest enough? Yup. So the alternative is to live alone until your face looks like a topographical map of the Himalayas. How's that sound? Okay, Okay, the red dress. And I added the heels.

Of course, Tony was exactly on time to pick me up. He wore a suit. A suit!

"You look nice," I stammered.

"So do you. I like your dress. I remember it from Cam's party."

"Thank you." We both seemed nervous and more formal than we'd ever been.

"I've made a reservation at Gino's. I've never been there, but my boss says they serve the best Italian food in town."

"Great."

We were quiet on the ride downtown, chatting intermittently about his work and my class. Avoiding anything substantive.

We were ushered to the only table decorated with pink roses. I glanced at Tony and he smiled when he saw me notice the flowers. "Tony, did you arrange for these lovely roses?"

"Yes, I didn't know if pink was the right color. Girls like pink, don't they?"

"They certainly do. Thank you." We both seemed a little more at ease.

After we ordered, Tony said, "Thu told me you two had a conversation the other day. I'm happy you're friends."

"I really like your sister. I trust her. And I'd like to know her better. She's a quiet woman, but sensitive and wise. She seems comfortable with me. Hopefully we'll be good friends over time."

"She told me about your offer to help her with English. That is very generous of you. You helped me with writing, and now you're helping my sister. I imagine you'll start with grammar?" He gave me his teasing look.

"Right. I think we'll start with negatives, learning the differences between "no, not and don't."

"I remember those lessons. It's very different for a Vietnamese speaker."

I suddenly had a brilliant idea. "Maybe Thu and I can exchange lessons. I'd love to learn some basic Vietnamese. Do you think she'd be willing to teach me?"

"Certainly. But are you a careful listener, Miss O'Neil?" he asked in a mock-stern voice.

"What do you mean?"

"Vietnamese is a tonal language. You must be able to differentiate tones in order to determine the meaning of a word."

"That will be a new experience for me. I've only studied Romance languages."

"I'm sure you'll be a brilliant student."

I looked at his face to see if he was being sarcastic, but his eyes were tender and sincere. "Thank you for your confidence."

He changed the subject. "Did I ever tell you how brave you were the night of Mr. Jones' attack?" We never talked about this incident.

"No."

"I was terrified when you asked that crazy man about fighting in Vietnam. I thought he might shoot Tran, then you." He paused and said in a shaky voice, "Escaping from Vietnam was easier than watching you and Tran with the madman. I still have nightmares about it."

I reached for his hand. He turned his palm up and gripped mine firmly and didn't let go until our salads arrived.

Tony began to talk about his plans. "Do you remember meeting Vi and William at the reunion?"

"Of course. The handsome couple in the import/export business."

"Yes. They are wealthy people. They may have told you they still do business in Vietnam, although some of the family resent them having anything to do with the present government. We can talk about that another time."

I was intrigued about doing business with the communist regime, but didn't want to interrupt his train of thought. Tony continued, "They have offered to loan me money so I can get through law school quickly and not have to work at the same time."

"How generous of them!"

"Yes, they are very good people. I'll repay them according to the note I've signed. And I've been awarded a scholarship from the Santa Ana Vietnamese community to help with tuition. William helped me with the application. I think he might have "hand-carried" my forms, as Americans say."

"How long have you been planning this?" I asked in amazement.

"For several years. I've saved part of my salary every month, but it hasn't been enough to support us if I'm in school full time."

He paused, looked down, then directly at me, I knew he was going to say something important. "And then I met you and wished I'd never made plans to leave."

My eyes filled. I couldn't help it. He squeezed my hand.

His voice was plaintive. "It's too late for me to change my plans, Callie. I've been accepted at school. I've arranged for loans. All I have left to do is find housing." Another pause. "And find a way to convince you to come with me."

"Oh, Tony. I'm so flattered and tempted, but I'm not free to do that. The Jones trial is coming up, and I'll have to testify. I can't leave Tom on such short notice. I own the condo. Then there's my writing class."

"I understand. But I need you to know what my perfect world would look like." The ESL teacher in me wondered at his absolutely appropriate use of "perfect world." Tony was thinking in colloquial English, no small feat. He impressed me in so many ways.

I needed to confide in him at that very moment. I wasn't sure why, but it was clear it was important to me and to us.

"Tony, my perfect world slipped away when I knew I wouldn't be a mother."

He stared at me, watching to see if I would expand on my statement. When I didn't, he said gently, "That makes three of us. You, Thu and me."

"Oh my god, it's true, isn't it? We share that loss." We retreated to our own thoughts for a minute. Then I asked, "Tony, did you ever love a woman you wanted to be the mother of your children?"

He squeezed his eyes shut and said very quietly. "Yes, there was a woman in Vietnam. We were neighbors. I think I loved her the moment we met, when we were children."

I waited, but he kept his eyes closed. "What happened?" I asked gently.

"She was killed during the war during a bomb raid. By an American fighter jet."

I felt I'd been slapped across the face. Both he and his sister had lost their lovers in the war. This time I reached for his hand, and he finally opened his eyes. I saw the pain and knew there was nothing I could say. We sat in silence for a few minutes, until our food was served. All of a sudden, I wasn't hungry.

"What about your husband," he asked. "Did you want him to be the father of your children?"

"Yes, I did. I always thought we'd have one or two children. But in our 30s, Paul drifted away from me. He said he never intended to have children. I think that was when our marriage really ended, although we lived together for five more years. I never felt the same about him."

Tony looked at his plate and pushed it away. "I didn't want this to be a sad night, Callie. I hoped our first real date would be happy."

"Me, too, Tony. But it seems we need to understand each other better before we can consider the future."

This seemed to cheer him up. It must have been my mentioning the future.

He said sympathetically, "There's no reason for us to rush, Callie. It's just that the timing is awkward with law school starting in a few weeks." I nodded in agreement.

To my surprise, he grinned broadly, "Callie, I have a crazy idea. Will you go back to California with me to look for a house? Wait, wait before you tell me you can't. We can fly and rent a car. I'd really like us to have some time alone together. I'll do some research about places for a wonderful weekend, so it won't all be work." He looked at me hopefully.

I couldn't help but catch his enthusiasm. Since I hadn't said no outright, he kept talking. "While I look for houses, maybe you could interview with the private language schools. What do you think?"

I couldn't think. I said, "Let me think about this, Tony, Okay?"

"Okay. Now let's get out of here. You can take the roses."

We left with Styrofoam containers of our untouched food and a plastic bag full of roses. What an amazing first date. I wondered what the second would be like!

Chapter 31

Back to California

This time, I needed my sister. Sharon and I talked regularly on the phone, usually about our mom and Sharon's teenaged girls, never about each other's personal lives. Sharon worked for IBM, and her husband was a banker. They were a very busy family. We shared holidays at their large home outside Chicago.

Sharon's voice was alarmed when she picked up the phone. "Are you OKAY?" Not hello, who's calling, or what's new.

"Yes, I'm fine. I just need to talk to you. I'm tired of talking to myself."

"How was the reunion?"

"It was amazing. And it's related to why I'm calling you."

"You've had a job offer in California and want to know if I think it's a good idea, right?"

"Sort of. Sharon, can you just listen for a minute."

"Of course I can. Sorry. Now tell me all about it."

I did, and she was quiet. I could hear her thinking and tapping something by the phone. I ended with, "I feel like I'm about to take a huge leap and don't know where I'll land." No response. "Sharon, are you there?"

"I'm here. I'm thinking. Give me a minute."

I waited. Her voice was gleeful. "Callie, it's been years since you've sounded so happy. I agree you shouldn't rush into anything, but I think you're in love!"

Now it was my turn to be silent. "Callie, Callie, are you there?"

"Yes," I whispered. Why did it take my sister to make me admit what had been happening for months? "You may be right!"

Sharon squealed. I hadn't heard that noise since we were kids. I doubted she squealed much at IBM.

"Callie, listen to me." I always did. She was older and bossy – in a good way. "Go to California with him. Spend some time alone. It sounds like there have always been family members around you two. Don't quit your job. Just have fun for a change."

"Okay, okay. Thanks, Sharon. I'll find a sub for my writing class. The trial won't be for another few months. I think I can swing it."

"What trial? What are you talking about?"

I had decided not to tell my sister or my mother about the Jones incident. What could they do? It was over. I gave Sharon a shortened version of the attack.

She gasped. "And you didn't tell me? Why, Callie? I don't understand."

I heard the hurt in her voice. "Because I didn't want to worry you."

Her IBM tone returned, no more squealing. "Let me get this right, a gunman grabbed a student, pressed a gun to his head, and your job was talking to him until the police arrived."

"Yes," I answered in the younger sister's voice from the past.

Now she boomed, "How could you think I wouldn't want to fly to you that night, to make sure you were cared for by someone who loves you? And to shoot the crazy fool! How could you?" she sputtered.

"Sharon, I was cared for by people who love me, and now that I think about it, I should have called you right away. I'm sorry."

"You're sorry. I'm sorry, too. There's something very wrong going on here. I obviously have been too busy with my own life to share in yours. That's my fault, and I'm going to fix it."

Oh no. When Sharon tackled a problem, there was no stopping her till she fixed it. And I appeared to be the problem. "Sharon, are you going to fly to California with Tony and me?"

She laughed. "No, but I'm going open an AOL account for you, then develop a fool proof plan for the two of us to spend time together. To heck with soccer league; to heck with technical conferences. Jim can take the girls somewhere when you and I escape. How does this sound?"

"What is an AOL account?"

"It's electronic mail, email. We can exchange messages any time, day or night."

I groaned, not Sharon at 3:00 a.m. She read my thoughts.

"Don't worry, it doesn't ring like a phone. I'll send you a computer with AOL installed and detailed instructions on how to use it. You'll love it, trust me."

"OKAY. As for our sister get-away, how 'bout we meet in San Jose? I bet there'll be some great Vietnamese restaurants we can try." She howled with laughter. Our conversation ended on a high note.

My first email would be to ask her not to talk to our mom about Tony until I was ready.

I felt much better after talking to Sharon. I skipped a conversation with the mirror and started to make a to-do list. First, find a sub to teach the writing class. Second, finish reading all the memoirs. This would take hours. Every student was into it! They submitted at least one essay a week. In Lien's case, up to three. I loved reading them and felt privileged to share their most precious memories.

Third, find time to talk to Cam. We hadn't caught up since the reunion. I wondered if she'd heard Tony's news. Or maybe he had shared his dream about law school a long time ago. I respected the way the Asian people I'd met kept confidences. I'm sure there was gossip, but I guessed that if you asked someone to respect confidentiality, they would.

*****

I called Tony after work the next day and told him I would go to California with him before school started. I heard the joy in his voice when he thanked me. We agreed we'd meet on the weekend to do some detailed planning.

What was I doing? The answer seemed to be exactly what my heart told me to do.

I pulled out my to-do list and dealt with the first item, find a sub for my writing class. I had met Lydia at a teachers' conference several years ago, and we had become friends. She had subbed for me when my mother needed post-surgical care, and the students loved her. She agreed to meet for lunch the following day to discuss teaching my writing class.

Lydia made a statement when she entered the restaurant. She wore her self-assurance like a cloak. Her long legs in black tights ended in high boots. Her bowler hat was tilted rakishly. Her make-up was dramatic, particularly the fire engine red lipstick. Her solid black hair was shoulder length, with carrot stripes in her bangs. It was a treat to see a 50-something year-old with so much pizazz. We hugged, then got right down to business.

I simply handed her one of Cam's and one of Lien's memoir pieces. As she read, her arched eyebrows shot up, revealing deep wrinkles in her forehead. She ran her hand through her perfect hair. "I'm astounded at this writing! Your students are spectacular. Are they all like this?"

I assured her I'd brought work from the two best writers, but that the others were also compelling. "Are you going to help them publish?"

I was taken aback. We had never discussed publishing. "Do you think there's a market for this content?"

"Duh, yes, there's a market," she exclaimed. "Let me tell you what I've been doing since we've seen each other."

"I'd like to hear. You're always up to something interesting."

Lydia managed to eat her Caesar salad while telling me about her contract with the publisher of educational books and teaching materials where she'd been working for the past nine months. "They're looking for meaningful content for ESL students, particularly for adults. Most of the traditional stuff is just plain boring and irrelevant to the students' lives."

She took a few more bites of lettuce before she continued. "You said you're going to LA?"

"Yes."

"The publisher is in Santa Monica, the west side. I'd like to introduce you to her. Her name is Denise Hernandez. You two will like each other, I'm sure. I think you could pitch a consulting contract using these memoirs."

I put my fork down and stared at her.

"What are you staring at, Callie?"

"Do you believe in omens?" I asked her.

"That depends on whether I like the coincidence or not. What kind of omen are we talking about here?"

"I can't go into details now, but I'm going to LA with a Vietnamese man I've been seeing. He wants me to move to LA with him, but I can't teach in the California public school system unless I'm certified by the State. He doesn't realize how poorly paid teachers are in private language programs."

"Aha, now I understand your omen question. Denise Hernandez may be your ticket to a different way to leverage your ESL skills. And you are a wonder, Callie. Do you know that?"

"Thanks, Lydia. I think the same about you." We both focused on eating a few bites. "Lydia, I would really appreciate an introduction to Denise. In the meantime, I'll approach my students about potentially publishing their memoirs. I think they'll be thrilled."

"Callie, I'll sub for you while you're in LA. How's that?"

"I owe you, Lydia. Let me buy your lunch."

"Now tell me about this man. He must be something to entice you out of your comfy life."

"He is, Lydia, he really is."

Chapter 32

South Pasadena

I returned the students' latest memoir pieces with my usual comments and suggestions. Jose's was so good, I asked him to read the first page aloud. He was thrilled to be the star that evening.

His subject was "coyotes" – people in business to smuggle immigrants across the border. Jose's memoir that night described how his parents entered through Arizona after paying a coyote every cent they had. Everyone listened in rapt silence to the harrowing story and clapped when he finished.

"Jose, that was excellent."

When he had returned to his seat, I began, "I want to include you all in a discussion about your memoirs." They looked at me intently. I explained that I would be meeting with a publisher of educational material in LA. Denise had been enthusiastic when I talked with her that morning, and we had set up an appointment.

"If you agree, I'd like to take samples of your writing to show to the publisher. If she thinks your work would be interesting to other students, she may pay you to publish your material."

They were silent. Cam was the first to react. "Yes, Callie, I mean Miss O'Neil. I would be so proud to publish my memoir. It would be good to be paid, but the honor would mean even more to me and my family." The others shared her sentiment.

I told them about my substitute Lydia, and they could hardly wait to meet her. I gave them a secret assignment. Write two paragraphs describing Lydia based on their first impressions, but not to show it to anyone until I return. They all laughed and promised secrecy.

I caught myself humming on the drive home that night. I'm normally not a hummer.

*****

Three weeks later, Tony and I landed at LAX. We both rented cars because each of us planned a busy afternoon. We checked into the Airport Marriott and agreed to be back at the hotel at six. Tony was meeting a realtor, and I was heading to Santa Monica. I had chosen ten excerpts from the memoirs to show Denise.

Denise was a slender, attractive blonde in her 30s, I guessed. She wore expensive slacks and a tailored white silk blouse. She made the outfit come alive with stunning southwestern turquoise earrings and several silver bracelets, some with inlaid stones. Her manner was both friendly and professional.

We talked briefly about my writing class. I handed her the samples and she started to read. She inhaled audibly and held her breath a few seconds. Then exhaled and gazed at me. "This is fabulous! Will you excuse me while I read the rest of them. Please help yourself to coffee or something cold. It's right out there."

I understood that she wanted privacy and obediently stepped toward the refrigerator in the adjacent room. Denise was either a slow reader or she was re-reading each piece. After finishing one bottle of water and half an orange juice, I returned to her office. She was scribbling furiously on the essays.

"Callie, there's something wonderful here. I have several ideas for using this content. I want to show these pages to my colleagues. May I do that?"

"Of course."

"We'll meet and discuss ideas, then ask you to come back. How long will you be in LA?"

"For ten days. When do you want to get together?"

"How about a week from today? That will give me time to show them to everyone here in Santa Monica and also in our New York office."

"Fine. I'm staying at the Airport Marriott. You can reach me there if you want to talk sooner."

I tried not to skip when I left the office. But as soon as I entered the elevator I hugged myself and let out a whoop. Denise loved the memoirs!

I called Cam from the car and told her. She started to cry and assured me they were tears of joy. She choked, "Have a wonderful time with Tony. You two deserve each other." She obviously knew. I could hardly wait 'til six to tell Tony.

In the meantime, I had two hours to kill. I consulted the rental car map and headed for Highway 101. During the reunion, we hadn't left Pasadena. This side of town was a totally different world, except for the palm trees.

Tattooed body-builders, skate boarders with purple hair, nearly nude teens with pierced body parts. I almost rear ended a car in front of me. You're not in Kansas anymore, I told myself. I drove north to Malibu and felt the serenity that only comes from watching the waves break on pristine beaches. It was time to turn around.

It took me 45 minutes to drive the last two miles on the 405 freeway. Where were all these people going? I looked for the terrible accident that must have caused this traffic, but only saw miles and miles of cars, barely moving. I was 30 minutes late to meet Tony.

He was waiting patiently for me in the lobby, and didn't mention the time. I apologized, explaining about the traffic. He placed his finger against my lips and led me to the elevator. When we entered our room, he took my hand gently and guided me to the bed. Our soft kisses lasted a few minutes. Then he slowly undressed

246

me. He kissed the soft skin on the inside of my arms. I wished I'd had time for a shower. But Tony didn't seem to care. In a few minutes, I didn't care either. I wanted him. I needed him.

We made love slowly, sweetly, like falling into water, and later passionately. His eyes were the color of fine maple syrup. We decided to skip dinner.

The next morning we showered together, something I hadn't done since Paul and I were first married. Tony meticulously washed my back and shampooed my hair. I did the same for him. We ordered room service for breakfast and ate dressed in identical terry robes.

Tony spoke softly, "Now I know why I left my country. I'm home now." He got up and kissed me gently. I felt tears of joy slide down my face.

When I had composed myself, I asked, "Do you have to be someplace today?"

"Yes, I have some houses to look at."

"Did you see anything you liked yesterday?"

"Not really. I need to be near a freeway or some kind of transportation to downtown LA. The realtor showed me houses way out in the Valley. I told her the commute would be too long."

We examined the map of Los Angeles together. I told him about my drive on the coast the day before and the wonders of humanity I'd seen. He laughed, then commented that finding a good neighborhood and school for Tran was important. We nixed Venice Beach.

He pointed to Santa Monica. "I wonder how long it would take to drive from there to downtown. I'll ask the realtor. It would be wonderful to live near the ocean. I agreed.

"What are you doing today, Callie? Have you followed up on any of the jobs I gave you?" I shook my head.

I hadn't told him the outcome of my meeting with Denise. Somehow, I wanted to be sure before getting too excited. But he searched my face and smiled. "What are you hiding, Callie?"

I couldn't keep a straight face. I told him about meeting with Denise. "Tony, she loved the memoirs! She wants to publish them. We're meeting in a week, and I think she'll have a proposal ready. I can't wait to tell the class. In fact, I already called Cam."

He pulled me onto his lap and kissed my neck. "You are a winner, Callie. My winner." The map fell somewhere on the floor.

It felt like a honeymoon. Tony called the realtor and postponed his appointment until after lunch. He asked her to show him houses in Santa Monica.

More room service. Another shower. Back to bed. When we heard the light tap on the door and "house KEEPING," Tony answered, "Just a minute." We hastily untwined and grabbed our robes. Tony opened the door just far enough to hand the pile of damp towels to the cleaning person and ask for a new supply, plus two extras. "Thanks, that's all we need." He carefully placed the 'Do Not Disturb' sign on the door and returned to me.

Finally, Tony looked determined. "I need to find a place to live. I can't find it from this bed, although I'd like to. I need to get dressed and remember why I'm in Los Angeles."

"Okay." I let him go, reluctantly.

"If you're not busy, will you come with me to look at houses this afternoon?" I agreed. I wanted to be with him. Even if he was just going to the cleaners. I knew I'd feel hollow without him.

We returned my rental car, and Tony drove us to Santa Monica. We looked at funky bungalows with handkerchief-sized patches of grass, gigantic three-story mansions, condos with ocean views and tiny rooms, and dingy apartments. Nothing suited, and they were all ridiculously expensive.

At dinner that night, I asked Tony about living in Orange County. "I've read there's a huge Vietnamese community there."

Tony's response was firm. "I'm not interested in living in Little Saigon for two reasons. First, I want to live in an American community. Second, the commute to downtown LA would be horrible."

"Okay." He had obviously considered and rejected Orange County. "How about Pasadena?" We looked on the map and saw it was just a little north east of downtown. "It's a pretty old city with some lovely Spanish-style homes. Didn't you think the area around

Cal Tech where my friends live is very attractive? I don't know anything about the schools, but Sal and Lou will."

We agreed that I should call my friends and ask them to refer us to a realtor. Sal's voice was surprised, "You're back in California! You just left."

"I know, Sal. Things have changed quickly. I'll tell you all about it. But right now, we need some advice."

"Who is we?" she asked.

"Tony and I are here together. He needs to rent a house while he goes to law school in LA. Do you know a realtor who could help us look in your area?"

"Of course, I do. But slow down, Callie. You and Tony are now 'we'?"

"Yes." I answered simply. Sal said nothing.

"Is he standing right there?"

"Yes," I repeated.

She laughed. "Okay. Can you two come to dinner tomorrow? I'll call a couple of realtors and let you know if they can give you a tour in the afternoon. Will that work?"

"Yes."

Sal laughed again. "You are very communicative today, Callie. Please don't say yes again." It was my turn to giggle.

"One more question, Callie. Is that attractive young boy who loves pickleball involved in the move?"

"Tran is Tony's cousin, and he is definitely part of the move."

"Then you have to look in South Pasadena or San Marino for a school. Tran will fit right in. The schools are full of brilliant Asians. They go to Stanford or UC Berkeley when they graduate."

"Not to Cal Tech?" I teased.

"Only the geeks."

"Thanks, Sal. We'll wait for your call."

*****

Tony fell in love with the second house we saw. An old Spanish two-story place, painted a sleepy shade of yellow. He loved the yawning entry way with its warm colored clay pavers on the entry floor, the archway leading into the dining room, the walk-in pantry, the small balcony outside the master bedroom, the chipped claw-footed bath tub, the tiny black and white tiles on the powder room floor, and especially the huge windows overlooking the Arroyo. Who cared if the paint was peeling off the shutters?

The house was furnished and had four bedrooms. Tony made me smile when he assigned the bedrooms. "Here's Tran's room. This one is Thu's. The master will be ours (another wink), and the fourth will be where I'll study. It's perfect, Callie."

The realtor explained that the owners were Japanese Americans, temporarily living in Tokyo where the husband had accepted a job with Toyota. They required a one-year lease. Tony signed on the spot.

We drove to Sal and Lou's under a gauzy LA sky. Sal rushed out to greet us and invite us in. Their house was cool and charming, decorated in southwestern colors – sand, mint, and burnt orange.

Tony brought out his map and pointed to Monterey Road where the house was located. Lou explained that we'd be living near the Pasadena freeway which was only nine miles long, but very, very busy at commute times. Tony asked if he could take the back roads downtown if the Pasadena freeway was too slow.

"Certainly," Lou answered in his professor's voice. "But Figueroa goes through East LA. You'd be driving through some pretty seedy neighborhoods."

Tony's face was neutral. "Lou, remember I've lived through a war. I can handle driving through East LA." No more was said about East LA.

I asked Sal and Lou about secretarial schools. Lou suggested we pay a visit to Pasadena City College. "In fact, it's only blocks from here. Would you like to take a walk and see for yourself?"

The campus was very near Cal Tech. Lou pointed out several new buildings. I spotted at least eight tennis courts and asked if there were pickleball courts, too. Sal smiled. "Funny you should ask. We've made a proposal to the City to convert two of the older courts to eight pickleball courts. Tennis is losing popularity and the courts are rarely full. In fact, they're practically empty in the afternoons."

Lou picked up from his wife. "On the other hand, pickleball is booming in Pasadena, South Pas, and Glendale. We need more courts." Tran would love that, I thought.

We picked up a catalogue from the Administration building. From a quick scan, there was a business program that might be perfect for Thu. She'd have to get a driver's license to get to school, but why shouldn't she? Everyone in California drove.

Tony wanted Sal and Lou to see the house he had rented, so after dinner we took a drive by. They congratulated Tony on his choice of location and explained that living by the Arroyo would be wonderful. There was a nine-hole golf course at the bottom, hiking trails, tennis courts, they went on and on. I wondered if they'd mention the coyotes and snakes that also enjoyed the hot, dry location, but they didn't. If they had, Tony would have reminded them that he came from Vietnam.

As we dropped them back at their house, Sal encouraged Tony to call her if he needed advice about the area or finding house repair people. We thanked them for a lovely evening. When we got into the car, I said, "Tony, I'm glad you'll already have friends nearby."

"I am, too. They seem like very kind people."

When we returned to the hotel, Tony was disappointed that it was too late to call Thu and Tran. "First thing tomorrow," he said. "They will love the house."

"Tony, let's spend tomorrow doing some research on secretarial schools for Thu and visit the middle school in South Pasadena."

"Fine. Good ideas. If there's time, I'd like to show you the law school." He grinned like a child, displaying perfect teeth, unlike his sister's. I wondered if Tony just had better genes or if Thu wasn't offered orthodontic care.

"I'd like to see it, Tony, so I can picture where you'll be."

Chapter 33

Decisions

Our mock honeymoon continued down the California coast, south of LA. Tony had booked us into the old Valencia Hotel in La Jolla. Our room provided a breathtaking view of the surf pounding the rocky coast. The mammoth window was framed in scarlet bougainvillea. I wanted a whole new round of Tony, room service and the view. That's pretty much what happened. Happiness sparkled from the ceiling, from the Jacuzzi tub and followed us everywhere.

We did get dressed a few times to stroll along and window shop in the upscale La Jolla town center – a charming place with art galleries, restaurants and clothes I'd never wear. Tony didn't seem to be much of a shopper, either.

On our second and last night in La Jolla, I thanked Tony for the spectacular weekend. "You were right, Tony. We did need time together, and I've loved every minute of it. It's been like a Hollywood honeymoon."

He pulled me to him and whispered, "I'd like our real honeymoon to be in Vietnam. Tran should come with us and visit his mother." I was startled and pulled back to see his face. He looked hopeful and apprehensive at the same time. "Is this another proposal?" I asked seriously. I pictured myself in an entryway, a little afraid to go in.

"Yes, Callie. I think we belong together."

I couldn't say a word, just put my arms around him and lay my head on his shoulder. He held my heart in his eyes.

"You notice I did not mention any time frame, Callie."

"Thank you," I said quietly. I felt so grateful that Tony made me feel cherished and serene. It was like a balloon full of rainbows had just popped in my heart. He was right, we did belong together.

*****

We returned to the Marriott for our last two days. I was excited the next morning as I dressed for the meeting with Denise. "Tony, would you like to come with me to the meeting?"

He was thoughtful, "If you'd like me there, I'd like to come."

"I'd like you there." And everywhere, I thought.

Denise was waiting for us in the outer office this time. She greeted Tony without questioning why he was there, and ushered both of us into a small conference room where two young men and one older woman were chatting. Denise made introductions, explaining that Katherine was the president of the company, and that Eduardo and Jon were technical writers and editors.

Katherine opened the meeting. "Callie, the samples you brought are marvelous. We have several ideas on how to use them. Here is a draft the four of us have been working on. Let's start with number 1." She was all business.

The meeting lasted two hours. The upshot was that the publisher wanted to "repurpose" the stories into reading material for adult English learners. They would break down the memoirs into small sections as topics for discussion. Students would then be assigned to write short memoirs of their own.

The second proposal was more exciting. Katherine would consider publishing the memoirs independently. They had a small division of the business that published non-educational books, mainly non-fiction. I couldn't help but interject how thrilled my students would be to actually have their work professionally published. "Could they include photos?" I asked.

Denise responded, "The more, the better." I didn't know if my class had photos, but it was worth asking.

Katherine smiled as she came to number 3. "Callie, please read along with me here. We would like you to join our staff as project manager of the memoirs. You're the perfect person for the job with your ESL expertise and your relationship with your students."

I was speechless. I had not anticipated number 3. Everyone was looking at me. Tony had taken my hand under the table, but his face was inscrutable.

I sputtered, "You want me to quit my job and work for you?"

Katherine laughed. "Correct, would you consider that, Callie?"

Everyone was looking at me, including Tony. I cleared my throat. "Do I have to answer right now?" My voice sounded childish.

"Of course not," Katherine responded. "I know this would be a major change in the direction of your career, but I think you might find it extremely satisfying. In the classroom, you are limited to reaching a few students. As a publisher, you can reach thousands."

"I'll keep that in mind, Katherine. When do you need a decision?" I hoped I sounded more professional.

"When you're ready. As long as it's within three weeks," she grinned.

Everyone started to get up when I thought of one more question. "Would you pay the students for publishing their work?"

Denise answered quickly, "Of course."

"Do you have any idea how much?"

"We're still in the preliminary design phase of the project, so we're not sure. But we are ready to use their content in text books immediately. If you need a number, what would your students think about $100 per essay? If we end up publishing their complete memoirs as books, we'd make a different financial arrangement."

"I think they would be thrilled with $100 per essay. But I should warn you. There are some prolific writers in my class. I can hear their brains ticking: if I write 3 essays a week, I'd earn $1,200 a month, $14,400 a year times ten years!" Everyone laughed.

Denise asked, "Do you need something in writing?"

Tony spoke for the first time. "Yes, I think Callie's students would appreciate a formal offer. And if I were you, I'd add a caveat that you need to approve the content as part of the acceptance process."

Katherine looked at Tony. "Are you a lawyer, Tony?"

He blushed. "Not yet, but I'm starting law school next month."

"You will do very well," she rejoined. Katherine turned to me. "We will also make you a formal offer, Callie. You should receive it at the end of the week. In the meantime, Denise, will you join me in my office. Callie and Tony, please wait just a minute longer." We sat back down, not having any idea what they were up to.

In five minutes, Denise returned and held out an envelope to me. "There are ten checks inside. Please add a name to each check and distribute them to the authors of the samples you gave us. And ask each author to sign the enclosed release form. Callie, please send us a list of each author's full name and contact information. They will join our list of contributors. Tony, you are welcome to review the release form before anyone signs."

"I've thought of one last question."

"Yes, Callie?" Katherine asked patiently.

"Do you use email in your company?" Everyone looked surprised.

Denise responded, "Yes, all the time. Particularly with our New York office, since they're in a different time zone. Why do you ask?"

"Well, I was thinking about my students. If I worked with them long distance, email might expedite the review process."

Katherine nodded, "An excellent idea, Callie. Do your students have computers?"

"I doubt it, Katherine. Perhaps we can find an inexpensive way to acquire them."

Eduardo jumped in. "Steve Jobs is giving computers away to schools in California. I bet Apple would be more than willing to expand their gifting program. Katherine, I'd like to volunteer to research this."

"Fine, Eduardo. Thank you."

Denise added an idea of her own. "Eduardo, if Apple isn't willing to help, I bet we could apply for a grant. There are several foundations dedicated to education. And the fact that these recipients are naturalized citizens would capture their attention, I'm guessing."

I wanted to squeal, but controlled myself. Tony and I thanked the group, shook hands and calmly left the office – until the elevator door closed. Then we kissed all the way down to the ground floor.

*****

On the flight home, Tony courteously avoided asking me about the publishing offer. We talked about his move, describing his new school to Tran, reporting to Thu about secretarial schools, and discussing the new house. Everything except my decision. I loved the fact that Tony didn't pressure me. I added patience to my mental list of his wonderful qualities.

When we ran out of practical topics, I asked Tony why he had chosen to be a lawyer. "I can't believe we've never had this conversation," I said to him.

"I don't talk about it much. But it's been my dream ever since I came to America. I want to specialize in immigration law."

That made sense. An immigrant who wants to help immigrants. "Please, tell me more."

"I will never live in my country under the communists. I want to help others escape to freedom. Not just Vietnamese people, but Chinese, Russian, Cuban – anyone who lives under communist rule. We all deserve to be free." He was quiet for a moment, then asked, "Have you ever heard about the 1965 Family Unification Act?"

"No, what was it?"

"It was passed to keep Asians from emigrating to the US. It stipulated that immigrants needed to have a family member already residing in the US in order to enter the country. At that time, two out of every three immigrants were European. And that's how Washington wanted to keep it."

I was surprised. "So how did it work?"

Tony smiled. "Asians in America were extremely creative, patient and determined to bring their extended families into this country. They offered to sponsor one family member after another until hundreds of thousands of Asians moved here. I guess you could say that the Reunification Act backfired."

"Will this law be important in your practice?"

"Absolutely," he answered solemnly.

"Are there law firms in LA that specialize in immigration law?"

"Yes, I've done a little research. But there appear to be more in San Francisco."

"Tony, are we already moving from LA to San Francisco?"

He laughed, "No, but you never know."

I had a glimpse of what our life might be like, tied more to ideals than real estate. Tony and Thu had moved several times already. What would prevent them from moving again? Then I asked myself, what would prevent you from moving? Nothing, absolutely nothing.

Chapter 34
Lien's Story

I was early for the first writing class since my return, but Cam was already waiting for me with a mischievous smile on her face as she handed me a manila envelope. I opened it to find the secret descriptions the students had written about Lydia.

"Callie, we decided to write them as a group, so we met after the second class with her. Each of us contributed at least two sentences.

I howled at the opening sentence. "Imagine a witty 60-year-old witch who shops in Macy's teen department."

"Oh Cam, you guys are wicked and terrific. I'm going to save these until I'm home, and I'll eat them like chocolates, one sentence at a time."

"How was your trip? I came early so we could talk."

I blurted, "Cam, I'm in love with Tony!"

She squealed (I'm not the only one) and enveloped me in a bear hug. "I'm so happy for both of you! I knew in California that he was already in love, but I wasn't sure about you. I'm not always good at reading emotions on American faces. You are an awesome couple. And Tran is so lucky. So is Thu."

"Cam, I'm really the lucky one. Tony comes with a built-in family of people I already love."

She frowned, "But what about your job? Tony's moving to LA, right?"

I sighed, "Right. That is a complication. But I think we can work it out."

Her voice wavered, "Does that mean you won't be teaching our class anymore?"

"If I move to LA, I'm afraid the answer is yes. But something wonderful has come up. I have a job offer from a publishing company in LA. I'll tell you and the class more about it tonight. They've offered me a position working with your memoirs. I think that means we can still collaborate on your book, just not in person every week."

Cam's smile was so huge her cheeks pressed her eyes into slits. She hugged me, then let go as the others trailed into the classroom.

Class was sort of a free-for-all that night. I listened to the stories about Lydia and how much fun everyone had with her. Several students submitted memoir pieces. But Jose broke the gaiety by standing and announcing formally, "Lydia is an excellent teacher, but we are all very happy you are home, Miss O'Neil." My eyes filled, and Cam gave me a sympathetic look.

"Thank you, Jose, and everyone." I took a deep breath, "Now seems to be the right time to tell you what happened on my trip." I explained about the job offer and the publisher's interest in their work. Their faces reflected sadness, then joy, then disbelief and elation when I distributed their first royalty checks.

They dutifully signed the release forms and printed their contact information on the pad I'd sent around. Lien asked carefully, "Then we will still be in contact with you, is that correct?"

"Yes, Lien, you may submit your memoir pieces to me as often as you wish. I'll review them and make suggestions. I'll keep the ones that fit into the curriculum and send you a check. I'm not sure about the publication process for your completed memoirs, but I'll certainly let you know."

She nodded her understanding, but the drooping corners of her mouth displayed her disappointment.

"One last thing," I looked at the familiar faces, already missing them. "Have you heard about AOL and email?" Only Jose nodded.

I continued. "It's a way to use computers to send messages to each other. We can type what we want to say, and also attach your essays. I can read them on the computer and send you my comments."

Cam said, "But we don't have computers!"

"We're working on that. Are you all willing to try?" Every head nodded.

The last few minutes of class were bitter sweet. I would miss these precious people but was delighted our relationship would continue, just not in the same way.

*****

I was too wound up to sleep that night, so I picked up Lien's next essay and was entranced, as I always was, with her bravery.

Two weeks after my daughter's birth, we were told that four Lutheran churches had agreed to sponsor us. They sent us airline tickets to Indiana. We were told that my other brother-in-law's family had moved to Illinois.

I didn't know that Indiana was a state. I thought we were being sent to live with Indians. My first thought was: am I going to eat corn the rest of my life? My second thought was: it's got to be better than living in the camp. I packed happily.

Bao slept most of the flight, but Dai was too excited to sit still. He wanted to visit the pilot, the toilet, have a drink, look out the window, etc. My nieces and nephew were a great help, squiring him around the plane, making sure he wasn't bothering the other passengers.

The flight was relatively short, but I was exhausted when we landed in South Bend. We gathered our carry-ons. My nephew slung mine around his shoulder. My oldest niece took Dai's hand and we slowly made our way down the jetway. The first thing we saw as we entered the gate area was a huge sign saying "Welcome to South Bend." At least 100 people were grinning and clapping as we stood, stunned by the crowd and their broad smiles and waves. They gathered around us, took our bags, shook hands, introduced themselves, hugged our children and kissed our cheeks. Our sponsors! Not an Indian among them.

The churches had rented us a four-bedroom house, furnished and stocked with canned food we'd never eat. During the months in camp, I had dreamed about having a real bed with a mattress where my sons and I could sleep. I vowed to sell food or anything I could find to save enough money for a bed. And here it was, a lovely bed that all three of us could sleep in.

Our house was near one of the churches. The pastor of this church and his wife became our main sponsor. My sister-in-law explained to them that I didn't know how to do anything domestic, so the pastor's wife became my home-making teacher. It wasn't long before I became competent at cleaning, doing laundry, ironing, and a little sewing. I never doubted I could care for my baby. After all, God had given me a brain.

Janet, one of the Lutheran ladies who loved to babysit for me, couldn't have children of her own. She asked me to give her one or both of my children, reasoning that I might want to start a new life on my own, since I didn't have a husband. I told her "No thank you." I didn't know if asking for someone's babies was customary in America.

There was no word from Van. We assumed that all high-ranking officers had been shot.

*****

I woke to the wail of sirens and immediately grabbed Dai and Bao and shoved them under the bed with me. I thought I was in Vietnam and we were under attack. Gradually, I became used to sirens and realized we were safe in Indiana.

We were busy, busy, busy. Church members were in our house every day. They escorted our children to doctors' appointments, dropped off the adults for checkups, arranged for job interviews for my in-laws and drove them to the interviews.

Our sponsors had thoughtfully prepared an album with church members' names and photos. Truthfully, we couldn't tell them apart. They were mostly white-haired elderly ladies with impossible names including Elizabeth, Priscilla and three Janets. We penciled in nicknames in Vietnamese by each photo to help distinguish one from another: big nose; lady with lots of makeup; large belly.

Every night, church members rotated baby-sitting responsibilities while the adults walked ten blocks to English class.

When the first snow fell, we all ran out to play in it, forgetting to bundle up in the coats, boots, gloves and scarves given to us. We were soon sick with colds.

The church members continually delivered canned food – something we rarely eat in Vietnam. We began to return the unopened cans to them and explained we just didn't like the taste. They slowly started to understand. After a few weeks, our sponsors delivered a case of soy sauce and huge bag of rice which delighted us. We were beginning to know each other.

The local butcher had been throwing away chicken feet and necks. He readily gave these parts to us so we could make chicken-rice soup. We consumed the soup every day until even we were sick of it.

When Bao was 18 months old, I entered junior college and studied computer programming. I earned an Associate degree in three years. I worked part time as a waitress some nights and weekends to earn money. The church ladies took care of my children.

One of the parishioners owned a two-bedroom house across from the church, and our sponsors rented it for me. We were grateful, and my brother-in-law's family understood our need for our own place.

I spoke Vietnamese to the children, but they were learning English very quickly.

Chapter 35

Moving

Back to school, I left a note for Tom, asking if we could meet after school. He responded with a note on my note, "Yes, how about 3:30 in my office?"

"How was California, Callie?" His voice was jovial.

"Wonderful, thanks. It's seems like ages since we've talked."

"I agree. I've missed you. Now what did you want to see me about?" Tom asked cordially.

I felt I was about to take a huge leap, perhaps over a cliff. In a paper thin voice, I started: "Well, Tom, I don't know how to tell you except to just say it."

His eyes narrowed, and his body went still. "I'm listening," his mouth a tight knot, expecting the worst.

"I'm in love with Tran's cousin, Tony. I plan to move to Los Angeles with them." My words felt shiny and new. I couldn't help smiling.

I'm not sure what he had expected me to announce, but he looked delighted. He stood up and stretched his arms out to me. I gratefully went to him and felt his kiss on my forehead.

"I will miss you very much, my dear Callie."

"And I, you, Tom." I brushed away tears I hadn't known were trickling down my face. "We've been a great team."

He nodded. "When do you want to leave?"

"As soon as you find my replacement."

"I'm not sure I'll be able to replace all the talent you've brought to this school, but I have a stack of applications to review, so go ahead and make your plans. Callie, you deserve to be happy."

My tears went from trickling to pouring, but I felt elated. I accepted Tom's handkerchief and apologized for the flood. "I must be pre-menopausal, Tom. Please forgive me."

He barked a laugh. "You haven't been in love for a long time. Enjoy every moment. Now go wash your face and call Tony with the news." He gently led me to the office door.

*****

Thu's voice on the phone sounded excited when she invited me for dinner that night. "What can I bring?" I asked her.

"You are family now, you can bring anything you want." Thu had never said this to me before. She had always formally refused all offers of help.

When I arrived, Tran answered the door. Without a word, he hugged me tightly and didn't let go for a long time. We didn't speak a word. I seemed to have spent a good part of the day crying, yet I felt overjoyed.

Tran led me by the hand into the dining room which was decorated with flowers, Vietnamese flags, American flags, and amazingly, a large dark brown stuffed bear sitting in a bowl in the center of the table. I had to laugh.

"Tran, who invited the bear?"

"The bear is the state animal for California. We tried to find poppies, but the florist didn't have any. She said they are like weeds. I don't agree, do you?"

"I'm with you, Tran, I love poppies, especially when orange and yellow ones grow together in a mass of color."

Tran's eyes sparkled, "Do you think they grow in South Pasadena?"

"I bet they do. They'll look gorgeous in a Spanish garden."

I followed the sound of Thu and Tony's voices speaking Vietnamese to the kitchen. "May I help?"

Tony wiped his hands on a towel and gave me a kiss, a real one. Thu stopped shredding lettuce and clapped, then hugged me and said, "Welcome, sister."

Tony smiled, "Yes, you can help. Will you slice up those limes?"

"What are we having tonight? It doesn't smell like stir fry."

Tran answered, "Tacos and beans. You can have fish tacos or beef tacos."

"May I have one of each?"

Tran's serious answer was "Of course you can." He sounded very adult sometimes.

"Tran, will you help me with something in my car?" I asked innocently.

"Sure," he followed me outside.

"I really don't have anything for you to help me with, I just wanted to talk to you alone." His face went blank. I recognized this was his wary look. His body became very still.

"We don't have time to drive to the school gym and sit on the bleachers and talk tonight." He smiled and his shoulders relaxed back to their natural position.

"What do you want to talk about?" he asked.

"I just wanted to ask if you're Okay with moving to Pasadena. I remember your story about living there with your aunt and hating it."

"Don't worry, Miss O'Neil. Tony and Thu won't make me sleep in St. Andrews church." Tran actually made a joke! I laughed.

"What about Hanna? Will you miss her?"

"Yes, but I'll find another girlfriend. I'm too young to get serious."

I struggled to keep a straight face. "That's true." I continued, "What about going to a new school?"

"You know I don't have any real friends at Acacia. Tony says there are lots of Asian kids in South Pasadena. I think I'll be much happier there. I may not even need to continue taking karate."

A second joke! "Tran, I think you are going to love South Pasadena. Your house is charming. Tony's already picked out a bedroom for you with a view of the Arroyo."

"I looked up that word and it means a dry gulch. Is that what it looks like?"

"Sort of. But there are lots of trees and scrub bushes. It doesn't look like Palm Springs, for example."

"Where's that?"

"Oh my, Tran, you have lots to explore in California. I think you'll love it. Should we go back now? Your cousins must be worried that I'm teaching you to drive."

He chuckled, "Wish it were true. Tony says everyone drives in LA. He said Thu has to get a license."

"How did she react?"

"At first she looked like she was going to faint, but Tony explained that she only had to drive around

Pasadena, so she felt better. I'm glad I don't have to teach her to drive."

Three jokes in one night. Tran was on a roll.

As we turned to go inside, Tran looked away and asked in a small voice, "Are you coming with us, Miss O'Neil?"

"Only if you promise to stop calling me Miss O'Neil."

Tran turned a bashful pink and whispered, "It's a deal, Callie."

The soft humid night caressed us as we walked back to the apartment, holding hands. The orange clouds skittered across the sky, like cobbled stones leading us home.

We normally drank iced coffee or tea, but tonight Tony uncorked a bottle of champagne. "Here's to a new life in California. For all of us."

We sipped and smiled. An amazing thought popped into my head. When had I told Tony that I would move with him? I hadn't! I was sure I hadn't. I told Tom and Tran, but not Tony.

Tony winked at me. He was getting really good at winking. "In case anyone here is wondering, Callie and I decided that she belongs in our family. We all love her and need her. We wouldn't be happy in California without her."

He explained to Thu and Tran. "Callie probably won't move as soon as we do because she has some things to finish up here, but we know she'll come as soon as she can." He looked at me, now winking, "Is that right, Callie?"

"That's right, Tony." My new family seemed to be coming together like four raindrops sliding down the window, merging into one.

*****

My sister Sharon's gift arrived by UPS a few days before Tony, Thu and Tran left for California. Just as she promised, there was a little message icon on the main screen. When I clicked on it, there was Sharon's message:

Congratulations, Callie! You've received your first email. I suggest you take the online tutorial to learn about AOL. I know you're going to love it.

I'm so happy you are moving to California. It will give me an excuse to visit you at Christmas. You'll be there by then, won't you? When is the trial? Has Tom found a replacement for you? How about your adult writing class?

Please send me your latest news.

XOXO,

Sharon

Tony, Thu and Tran were intrigued with my new toy. Tran seemed particularly fascinated. "Callie, do you think I could send messages to Hanna on email?"

"If she has an account, I'm sure you could."

Tran turned to Tony, "Do you think we can buy a computer, Tony?"

Tony smiled. "Yes, Tran, I think I'll be using one in law school and also for keeping in touch with Callie. Let's see about one right away to be sure it will work with Callie's. My last day at work is on Friday. We can go to Radio Shack on Saturday." Tran was delighted.

Thu surprised us by joining the conversation. "I think I'll want a computer of my own for business school. I took typing in high school and think that having computer skills will be important for finding a new job."

We all looked at her in amazement. I wanted to encourage her. "Thu, you are absolutely right."

She smiled shyly, but stuck to her guns. "Tony, I'd like to come with you and Tran on Saturday."

He patted her shoulder and said, "Of course."

So two computers were packed carefully into Tony's car when they left for California that weekend. We had tested out messaging and been delighted to hear a voice telling us, "You've got mail." Tony promised to send me a message every day. I said I'd do the same. Nevertheless, I couldn't keep my tears from streaming as they drove out of town.

I was deposed for the Jones trial soon after they left. Tran was deposed in Los Angeles, with Tony at his side. Collin Jones was declared unfit to stand trial and was sent to a hospital for the mentally ill. Aside from having to relive the terrifying attack, the incident faded in comparison to the changes coming up in my life.

Tom had found someone to take my job at Acacia. And Lydia had agreed to teach my advanced writing class for the first semester. The students were delighted. Cam hosted a welcome party for Lydia and a good-bye party for me. Each student composed a special message for me, mostly thanking me for my support and encouragement to write their memoirs.

Eduardo had been successful in locating free computers for the class. Their first lesson was the week I was leaving. We all sent messages to each other, some of which were worth keeping. So we learned to archive them for later use in the students' essays.

The fact that I'd be in touch with them made the last class far easier. That and Lydia's outrageous outfit that featured an orange jump suit with high-heeled purple boots.

The first messages from Tony, Thu and Tran arrived as soon as they moved into the Monterey house. Tony wrote that Sal and Lou had invited them to lunch, then to play pickleball. Tran was excited to meet a group of kids his own age at the courts, including several Asians. They told him he could choose to play at pickleball during PE if he wanted.

Tony also said that Thu had signed up for accounting class at Pasadena City College and had already been to the first class. "I took her driving and was scared to death because she tends to drive far too close to the cars on the right. I was squirming the whole time and trying to appear calm. I understand there are driving schools that will teach her. I think that's the right answer. Unless you want to teach her when you get here." He added, "Thu is very determined to drive, which is a good thing, I think. I need to look into insurance right away."

I laughed at the fear imbedded in his message and wondered if I'd be a more relaxed teacher. We'd see.

The most surprising message came from Thu two weeks later.

Dear Sister,

I love my accounting class. The instructor, Mr. O'Brien, is very kind and patient. He says I have a gift for numbers and a logical mind. I am very pleased. I'm learning to drive, which is difficult – terrifying is what Tony told Tran. I think Tony is very nervous teaching me. Maybe you can help.

I want to take Business English, but will wait until you are here and can help me. I have not forgotten our promise to teach our languages to each other. I am looking forward to teaching you Vietnamese.

One last thing that will surprise you. I'm going to wear braces on my teeth. Vi and William have offered

to pay. I will repay them when I get a job. I have always been embarrassed by my teeth. I will feel more American if I have a nice smile like yours. My first appointment is next week.

Please come soon.

Tom drove me to the airport exactly four weeks after Tony, Thu and Tran started their new life in California. I could hardly wait to see them and start work at the publishing house. I was very excited about my new life and told myself to ignore the flu I must have caught right after Tony left. It was good my seat on the airplane was near the restroom. I tried to focus on the bloated clouds outside my window seat.

BABY

Callie O'neil Vong and Tony Vong
are thrilled to announce the birth
of their daughter
SHELLEY THU WONG
reception at the home of Shelley's
Godparents Vi and William Mai
October 1, 1997
941 Their Street
Santa Monica, CA

Chapter 36
Shelley's Story

My mom calls me her miracle baby. She cries every day when she counts my toes, but she's smiling when she gets to ten. I only cry when I'm hungry. My brother Tran never cries. My dad smiles all the time, except when he's studying, which he does a lot. He's getting ready for a big exam.

Tran and his friends push my stroller down the Arroyo. We've seen coyotes and foxes, lots of lizards and birds. I love it when he pushes really fast. Sometimes Tran's girlfriend, Lisa Chang, comes with us. She's beautiful, but Tran says he likes her because she's smart. They are in the gifted program together.

On the weekends, when Mom is home from work, we all walk around South Pasadena. Auntie Thu and her special friend Ken O'Brien often go with us. I sleep in Auntie Thu's old room since she moved into her own place.

Tran often creeps into my room after I've gone to bed. I feel very happy when I wake up and see him sleeping there. He is my best friend.

Afterword

Tony and Callie lived happily ever after in Southern California, although his law practice took him to San Francisco and Vietnam. Six of them traveled to Vietnam to visit Tony's and Thu's mother – Tony, Callie, Thu, and Tran – Shelley and Ken O'Brien (soon to marry Thu) were numbers five and six.

Unknown to anyone, Tony kept a diary. Here's the entry that preceded their trip.

At 4:00 a.m. one morning, I received a phone call. A soft voice said in Vietnamese, "This is your mother speaking." We spent the next 15 minutes crying together. I finally asked her how she had managed this call. She said she had helped a U.S. man find a way to marry the Vietnamese woman he had fallen in love with. In exchange, my mother asked him to help her find her son.

The man searched through telephone books and called every number with our name until he found me. He then asked a friend in Canada to put the call through.

She explained that she had taken a job at a food export company. She saved enough to order a

refrigerator from the Sears catalogue. After the war, she
supported herself and my siblings by selling ice cubes on
the street.

Callie was instrumental in getting Cam's, Lien's and Jose's memoirs published as the first three autobiographies in the publishing company's series on immigrants.

Thu became Mrs. O'Brien. Her smile was stunning after the braces were removed. Her driving record is flawless, which could be explained by her practice of staying under 30 miles an hour and never driving on freeways.

Tran became a junior pickleball champion and played competitively in school and as an adult – right up to shoulder surgery, from which he eventually recovered. His partner on and off the court is a fellow attorney he met at UCLA law school. She's a brainy beautiful Jewish girl whom Callie and Tony adore.

Lien fell in love with an American and had been happily married to him for two years when she received a call from Quan, her ex-brother-in-law. He gave her amazing news – Van had not died, but somehow lived through more than a decade in hard labor in a "re-education" camp. Quan visited him in Hanoi when he was released (thanks to John McCain) and described how devastatingly shrunken and ill Van appeared.

Quan conveyed a message from Van to Lien, "I still love you and want to reunite our family." Lien was shaken to the core. Her husband gallantly agreed to whatever arrangement she decided was right. Lien reassured him that she would never leave him, but that Van should at least have a relationship with his children.

Months later, when Van traveled to Illinois to stay with Quan, Lien's children reluctantly flew to meet their father. The children didn't speak Vietnamese, and Van didn't speak English. Quan acted as interpreter. The visit was miserable for everyone.

The children's relationship with their father eased somewhat over time, but was never close or comfortable. Van eventually married a Vietnamese woman and returned to live in his native town.

Shelley is a love child, still a work in progress. Tran has appointed himself her protector for life.